Anonymous

Some Reflections upon the Prerogatives, Power and Protection of

St. Joseph

spouse of the blessed and ever immaculate Virgin Mary, Mother of God - with

several devotions to the said most glorious patriarch

Anonymous

Some Reflections upon the Prerogatives, Power and Protection of St. Joseph
spouse of the blessed and ever immaculate Virgin Mary, Mother of God - with several devotions to the said most glorious patriarch

ISBN/EAN: 9783337303068

Printed in Europe, USA, Canada, Australia, Japan

Cover: Foto ©Andreas Hilbeck / pixelio.de

More available books at **www.hansebooks.com**

REFLECTIONS

UPON THE

PREROGATIVES,

POWER and PROTECTION

OF

St. *JOSEPH,*

Spouse of the blessed and ever immaculate
VIRGIN MARY MOTHER OF GOD;

WITH SEVERAL

DEVOTIONS

To the said most glorious PATRIARCH.

He who is the Keeper of his Lord shall be glorified.
Prov. xxvii. 18.

LONDON:

Printed by J. P. COGHLAN, No. 37, Duke-Street,
Grosvenor-Square.

M,DCC,XCI.

THE

PREROGATIVES,

POWER and PROTECTION

OF

St. *JOSEPH.*

CHAP. I.

Of the Dignity and Glory of St. Joseph.

NEVER did any perfon, of what rank foever, claim with greater juftice, the fublime encomium, *Her Hufband is noble*, Prov. xxxi, 23, than the Virgin Spoufe of *Mary*. He was moft noble by his birth, noble for his merits, noble in his ftation. The mifcalled Grandees of the World too frequently raife themfelves by rapine and blood, on the ruins of oppreffed innocency; they aggrandize themfelves, ftanding above the vulgar, upon a high pedestal of riches and titles, which to the moral Philosopher, Seneca. Epist. 41. appeared no greater a wonder than to admire a *pigmy* upon a mountain; bring him down, and the dwarf is matter of mirth: In like manner, divest those who are adored, of what so highly recommends them, and they may be in the lamentable circumstances of trampled on *Sejanus*, or starved *Belisarius.* The mighty Conqueror of *Asia*, *Alexander* stiled the *Great*, made a blaze, *the Earth was silent in his Sight*, 2 Machab. i. 3. he pushed on his conquests to the extremity of the earth, and slaying Kings and Princes, he vanished upon the sudden, little remaining of his memory, except the invading others dominions, and generous answers, kind Historians allow him, in entertaining friends or enemies.

There is a noble sort of *Grandeur*, viz. *Virtue*, *which raises a man above the level of others, and places mortals above the stars*; Senec. Epist. 88. This looks on earth with dif-

'ory.

es and
hiluſo-
red no
ıdmire
bring
tter of
thoſe
highly
ıay be
es of
l *Beli-*
or of
made
in his
:d on
ıf the
nces,
little
ıt the
d ge-
ıs al-
ls or

ıdeur,
mun
places
Epiſt.
diſ-

dain, and aſpires to be called great in the kingdom of heaven. St. Mat. v. 19. St. Joſeph was favoured with all requiſites, to render him thus truly *great.* By birth he was a prince lineally deſcending from the renowned kings of the written Law; he had in his veins the pureſt blood of ancient Patriarchs and Prophets. The Evangeliſt brings down his predigree from great Abraham, and the angel ſalutes him with the royal title, *Son of David. St. Mat.* i. 20. Not to dwell upon this unparalleled extraction, he had the ſame progenitors as the Son of God made man, and the ſeveral promiſes of God to the houſe of David, 2 *Reg.* 7. 8. *Reg.* 9. *Pſalm* lxxxviii and cxxxi. of the expected Meſſias to be born of his race, and to be called King of the Jews, (as he was ſtiled in the grot of Bethlehem) *St. Matt.* ii. 2. devolved to our Redeemer from St Joſeph.

It would be reviving the blaſphemous hereſy of ſtigmatized Cerinthus, to aſſert, that Jeſus was by nature the real Son of Joſeph, yet he muſt be looked on as his legitimate parent,

A 3 and

and entitled in all things to the right of paternity, except that of genera-tion, *Damascen. Orat. de Nativ. B. V.* which according to Rupertus Abbas, *Rupert in 1 Math.* the eternal Father supplied, by infusing into the husband of Mary, a paternal love for her Son Jesus. *Rupert ibid.* A child lawfully conceived in matrimony, may strictly call the husband father, which title the Holy Ghost honors St. Joseph with, by the mouth of the immaculate Vir-gin in her blessed Son's presence: *Your father and I have sought you sorrow-ing. St Luke* ii. 48. Children reputed by common fame to belong to such a parent, or those who are adopted, have a right to inherit titles and pa-trimonies; much more Jesus who was born of Mary, Joseph's wife; for ac-cording to the approved axiom of the law, *Whatever grows in, or is built upon another's soil, belongs to the owner thereof; Instit. de Rer. Divis.* nor doth it invalidate what is here offered, that Jesus was the supernatural fruit of virginity; for a corn growing mira-culously in a field, belongs to the

owner

owner of the soil. In like manner Mary was the real mother of Jesus, miraculously begotten and miraculously born, and Joseph by matrimonial right may term him Son, because born of his wife's body. The sceptre of Juda usurped by invading and intruding Herod, came to Joseph by hereditary succession, and consequently to Christ, verifying what the Archangel foretold, *St. Luke* i. 32. *The Lord will give him the seat of David his father.* Fervourous contemplatives may address St. Joseph, with the admiring expression of old Tobias to the Archangel Raphael, *You are come of a noble race! Tob.* v. 19. What is yet more glorious, St. Joseph had the honor to call him Son upon earth, whom the first person of the adorable Trinity, has owned from all eternity his begotten Son.

When the Almighty deputed Moses to bring his chosen people out of Egyptian slavery, and to humble and confound the tyranizing Monarch, he favoured the Thaumaturgus with the glorious title, *I have appointed thee*

A 4 *the*

the God of *Pharoah, Exod.* vii. 1. that as by *eminent power, Corñel a Lap hic,* to terrify him with afflicting prodigies. After a more indulgent manner, he might be called the God of the *Hebrews, protecting, conducting, governing and ſupporting them. Idem ibid.* By the ſame rule, what may not be ſaid of the grand Patriarch St. Joſeph? who conducted, protected, governed and ſupported the God of Moſes? He out of all the Tribe of Juda was ſelected, *as a conſort and comfort to the mother of Chriſt, the moſt faithful and ſole codajutor to Jeſus in his great council upon earth.* * *If he who receives a Prophet, in the name of a Prophet, ſhall have the reward of a Prophet;* † He who with toil and ſweat, entertained *God made Man,* ſhall not he have a reward proportionable to the greatneſs of his gueſt? His daily actions in ſerving Chriſt, related to the order of hypoſtatical union, and therefore were more di-

* S Bernard hom. 2 Super Miſſus eſt.
† Mat. x. 41.

vine

vine. * Can any thing be more aftonishing, and at the same time more delightful than a reflection, how Joseph walked with Jesus in one hand, and Mary in the other, both being committed by heaven to his care and conduct.

The Omnipotent, who with lightning, thunder, and dreadful sound of trumpet, proclaimed a strict command; *Honour thy father and mother, Exod.* xxiii. 12. doubtless, was the most exact obferver of it, and confequently refpected St. Joseph, next to his virgin Mother. The deference of provoked Coriolanus to his mother Volumnia, *Val: Max.* l. 5. c. 4. and the tendernefs of Æneas to his father Anchifes, are but faint refemblances of Jefus's love to Jofeph. He who

---

* A Lapide in 1 Matth.

Qædam minifteria præcife pertinent ad ordinem gratiæ gratum facientis, & in hoc, fupernum faftigium tenet Apoftoli, &c. alia vero funt minifteria, quæ attingunt ordinem unionis hypoftaticæ, qui ex fuo genere profectior eft, ut patet de maternitate Dei in B Virgine, & in hoc ordine eft minifterium S. Jofephi. Suarez 3. Queft. 29. Difput. Sect. 1. 8.

said

faid, long before the incarnation, *I am God and not man,* *Ofee* xi. 9. honored him with divine affection. A dutiful child never loved fo intenfely. He loved him as a vigilant preferver of his life, withdrawing him from the bloody hand of perfecuting Herod. If Mardochæus for detecting the confpiracy of Bagathan and Thares, againft king Affueres, deferved to have that dutiful performance tranfmitted to posterity by imperial annals, *Efter* ii. 21. to be cloathed with royal robes, and a princely diadem fet on his head, the firft Prince of the court to lead his horfe, through the large ftreets of populous Sufan, and to proclaim; fo *the man is to be honored, Ibid.* c. vi. 8, 9. *whom the King is pleafed to honor;* what preferment, what marks of efteem and glory, is due to our great Patriarch the guardian and governor of the King of Kings, Jefus Chrift, who fupported him in his minority, and with many a fatiguing day's work, took pains, that the Son of God fhould not be neceffitated to pafs from door to door begging fubfiftence? All the noble precedents, of grateful return to favours, recorded by Plutarch, Titus Livius, Val. Maximus, and other authors, whether facred or profane, are infignificant and ufelefs, to exprefs Jefus's love to Jofeph. Hear our bleffed Redeemer's own words in a revelation approved by the Eaftern Church, and recited by Ifidorus out of grave authors; *I converfed (faid Chrift) with Jofeph, as if I had been his fon, he commanded me and I obeyed him, I loved him as my father, and even as the apple of my eye.* So was he honored, whom the great God of Affuerus was pleafed to honor; the Omnipotent *Creator obeyed the voice of man Jof.* x. 14.

The Apoftles took it as a fpecial favor, to eat at the fame table with their Meffias and Mafter, and certainly it was fo: the penitent Magdalen diffolved into tears of love at the kiffing his facred feet, her foul overflowing with heavenly delights; St. John Evangelift leaning on his divine breaft feemed to have a fore-

tafte

taste of the sweets of Paradise; and yet what is all this, compared to the privileges St. Joseph enjoyed, not for a short time, but conversed familiarly with him, for the long space of near thirty years? The little Jesus in his infancy leaned daily on his father's breast, and whilst the Patriarch humbly caressed him, it is no vain imagination to represent to ourselves the divine babe stretching forth his sacred arms, casting them about his neck and saluting him. Oh! the unspeakable joy, which then replenished the heart of this blessed Saint! especially at such times as deputed choirs of angels sung in the little house of Nazareth the glory of their great God there present in St. Joseph's arms. This happened frequently as the blessed Virgin revealed to St. Bridgit in the following words; *St. Joseph often beheld an admirable glory, in the midst of which my Son appeared in great splendor, and at the same time heavenly music delighted our hearts, the angels declaring and singing the glory of my Son.* St. Bridg. lib. 6. Rev. c. 58. St.

Joseph

Joseph kissing a thousand times the sacred feet of his Saviour, seemed continually on Mount Thabor, and had the greatest reason to congratulate with himself, and say to Jesus, *Lord, it is good for us to be here. St. Matt.* xvii. 4. The hidden life of Jesus of Nazareth, is a subject, not for discourse but contemplation.

The merciful decree having passed to redeem prevaricating mankind, the Son of God singled out the ever immaculate Virgin Mary to be his mother, whom the eternal Father adopted as his daughter. A *consort* was to be found, a *helper like to herself,* Gen. ii. 18. and for many important reasons. That she might not be stoned to death for an adulteress, that her pedigree might be derived by her husband's, that she might have a support and comforter. St. Ignatius M. adds a fourth, *Apud. S. Hieron in* 1 *Math:* That the miraculous conception of Christ *might be concealed from the Devil.* But seeing *that man is head of the woman, as Christ is head of the Church —and as the Church is subject to Christ,* ſo alſo women in all things to their huſbands. *Ad Epheſ.* 5. 23, 24: Who was ſo qualified as St. Joſeph to command her whom the higheſt Seraphim whould take it as an honor to obey? She to receive ſubmiſſively a huſband's orders, and to move immediately at his firſt beck; hear and admire! The moſt bleſſed Trinity, out of the numerous Tribe of Juda, made choice of the Heir to the crown and ſceptre of David, *Rupertus. Corn. a Lapide in* 1 *Math.* poſſibly not becauſe he was ſo, but for that he was juſt, *St. Mat.* i. 19. which word is comprehenſive, and includes, *a perfect poſſeſſion of all virtues, S. Hieron. in* 1 *Math.* If men of the world could have appointed their parents, they would have had them ſo poliſhed in every reſpect, that the moſt inventive thought could not deſcribe perſons of greater perfection both as to mind and body; the power of God could make the ſpouſe of Mary preferable in virtues to all other men, and to ſurmiſe his goodneſs has not favored him, is to rank divine affection beneath our own.   We

We cannot be too tender and cautious in the least seeming comparison, relating to the blessed Virgin with St. Joseph. She is like the radiant sun; in her presence stars of the first magnitude disappear. She alone gave a body to redeem the world, *for the flesh of Christ is the flesh of Mary. S. Augustin, Serm. de Assump.* The omnipotency of God *cannot create a greater mother. S. Bonav. l. 2 in spec. B. M. S.* She had a clear knowledge of all her emident dignity; that she was not only sovereign Queen of all Saints and Angels, but the true and real Mother of God. And in this respect St. Joseph was much her inferior, yet the love and respect she had for her dear Spouse, caused her to set aside her prerogatives, and as one under obedience, to render him all manner of service and honor imaginable. Jesus was her God, and she called Joseph her Lord, *(Bridg. 7. Rev. c. 25.)* speaking to him and of him with profound respect and esteem, as if he had been more deserving than herself. Never was any Virgin

Lady so faithfully loving, so chastely behaved, so religiously engaging in conversation, with her noble Spouse. She loved him tenderly, as the zealous protector of her consecrated virginity, as the preserver of her unspotted honor, against any surmise or reproach, concerning her virginal child-birth: she respected him as head and husband, as one of the greatest merit of all mankind, next to her Son Jesus; therefore she chearfully condescended to the meanest services, whereby she could express her humble duty. O prerogative not to be sufficiently set forth by an Angel! If the astonished St. Elizabeth was fixed in admiration, and with a loud voice, cried out, *whence is this to me, that the Mother of my Lord should come to me. (St. Luke* i. 43.) how ought we to extol his dignity, whom the same Mother of God served and obeyed thirty long years? The devout clients may take full notice, how in honoring St. Joseph they join with the ever blessed Virgin, in her former frequent performances.

We

We are not to difcourfe of St. Jofeph in the fame dialect, as when we mention other faints. The eternal truth indeed has declared, *that among the born of women, none has rifen greater than John the Baptift,* St. Mat. xi. 11. which at firft fight, feems to poftpone the bleffed Virgin; St. Luke explicates the foregoing words. *There has not arofe a greater prophet. (St. Luke* vii. 28.) Hence St. Ambrofe and St. Hilarius obferve, that the Baptift is not ftiled greateft abfolutely but relatively to the Prophets of the Old Teftament. He is not compared to the bleffed Virgin, St. Jofeph, or the Apoftles, *who following Chrift by reafon of their apoftolical dignity were not lefs, perchance greater than John. (Corn. a Lap in Math.* 11.) Be it how it will, in refpect of the firft evangelical promulgers of Chriftianity, *t at prudent and faithful fervant whom our Lord conftituted over his family to provide food in due time, (St. Mat.* xxiv. 45.) in all equity feems excepted from the general rule. Let it be fpoken with
all

all imaginable deference to St. John, the zealous priest, undaunted prophet, and glorious martyr, there appears a vast distance betwixt a parent and precursor. The blessed Virgin Mary, *as Mother of God, has a certain infinite dignity*; *(St. Thom.* 1. p. q. 25.) next to her the greatest degree of honor seems St. Joseph's right, *by as much as he was raised to higher dignity* above others. *(St. Tim.* 3. p.) What St. Mathew sets down; *Mary of whom Jesus was born*, is to contemplatives, a compleat elogium of all her praises. St. John Damascen makes the same inference as to St. Joseph, *for calling him the husband of Mary, the title is ineffable, (Con.* 3. *in nat. B. Maria,) and nothing more glorious can be said of him.*

St. Joseph's personal services to God made man, and those of the blessed Virgin, are of a far higher rank, than what was performed by others.

He laboured, he toiled, that our blessed Redeemer might be supported and supplied in all human necessities:

so that at the last dreadful day, when the wicked men *will wither away with fear.* (*Luke* xi. 26.) whilst happy souls will be admiring the goodness of the immortal Judge, for taking notice of their small duties in relieving him, in the persons of his *little ones,* as not knowing well how to understand the superlative favor, they will inquire, Lord! When did we see you *hungry, naked, or a stranger* (*St. Mat.* xxv. 34. 35.) at that time our great Patriarch, may receive public honors before the congregated universe; for whereas our merciful Saviour will say to the lowest saved souls, *come ye blessed of my Father,* &c. the charming and glorious acknowledgment, may be literally applied to St. Joseph after this manner, *Come my blessed Father, take possession of a kingdom prepared for you from the beginning of the world, for I* (who sit on this throne) *was hungry, and you gave me to eat, thirsty and you gave me to drink, a stranger and you entertained me for thirty years in Egypt and Palestine.* If St. Martin, when a Catechumen,

deserved

deserved to see Christ, bearing on his sacred shoulders part of the cloak he had bestowed upon an indigent creature, *(In vita S Martin.)* we cannot comprehend the honors reserved by the great and good God, who with sound of trumpet may proclaim, I was naked from head to foot, and Joseph here present cloathed me, he frequently divested himself of his own garments to secure me from shivering, in freezing blasts.

The mellifluous doctor of Claravallis makes a sort of a parallel betwixt Joseph the son of Jacob, governor of Egypt, *(S. Bernard, Hom. 2. in missus est)* and Joseph governor of Christ. The second has stricter right to the encomiums of the first, attributed to him in sacred writ. *No man on the earth,* says Ecclesiasticus, *Ecclef.* xlvi. 17. *was like to him, was a man born the prince of his brethren, the stay of the nation, a prop of his people:* the Egyptian monarch took the ring from his own finger and gave it into Joseph's hand, ordering him to mount the *second chariot, (Gen. iv.)* commanding all

all *to bow the knee before him,* and a
crier to proclaim, that *he was governor over the whole land of Egypt,* the
throne only diſtinguiſhing him from
Pharaoh, who ſaid of him; that he
was *full of the Spirit of God.* Gen. xlii.
The application is obvious. The
ſpouſe of the bleſſed Virgin was a
prince choſen by the Almighty to be
the ruler and ſupport of the ſacred
family, he was honoured with the
moſt glorious wedding ring, as huſband to the Mother of Jeſus, in all
probability having the ſecond ſeat in
heaven, next to his virgin ſpouſe. He
was the protector of his Saviour, and
by conſequence *full of the Spirit of
God;* for, doubtleſs, the Holy Ghoſt
co-operating ſo immediately to the
incarnation, deſcended upon him as
he did upon the apoſtles, as far as was
expedient to diſcharge his incumbent
duty, bleſſing him with angelical purity, ſingular prudence, heroic fortitude, unlimited patience, unſhaken
conſtancy, profound humility, ſera-
phical love of God, and intenſe affection for his immaculate ſpouſe, as alſo
ſuch

such other virtues as seemed due to him, who was deputed not to prevent famine in Egypt, but to preserve the *Bread coming down from heaven,* (1 *Joan.* vi.) which was to redeem mankind, and nourish the faithful, in the blessed sacrament of the altar, rendering them happy in paradise by the beatifical vision of himself, and the other two adorable persons of the most sacred Trinity.

From what has been already offered, may con-naturally be inferred, that *it is not temerarious nor improbable, but rather pious and very likely to be of opinion, that S. Joseph excels all other saints* (except the blessed Virgin) *in grace and glory. Suarez p.* 3. *t.* 2. *Disput.* 8. *&c.* None can dispute precedence of coronation with the royal consort of the Mother of God. Marcianus, a servant and subject, became emperor upon the marriage with Pulcheria, they both living virgins; and it would be a defect in judgment as well as in devotion, to entertain a thought that others go before the Favourite of Heaven. The consulting sedate reason and common sense lays demonstration in our way, that lower subjects gives place to him, who was the object of Jesus's and Mary's ardent affections: so that the dream of Joseph in Canaan is verified also in our glorious Patriarch, *the stars adore him, Gen.* xxxix. 7.; that is to say, all blessed spirits reverence him, as was revealed to S. Gertrude on the Vigil of the Annunciation of the blessed Virgin, to whom heaven was laid open, and when the choir sung S. Joseph's praises, or the priest at the altar named him, the saints bowed their heads, *(In vita S. Gertrud)* shewing signs of joy, and congratulation, for the honours done him upon earth. Wherefore as the worship of Latria is offered solely to God, Hyperdulia to the blessed Virgin, the highest Dulia belongs to S. Joseph.

Before I close this chapter, I cannot forbear remarking how unjust the common pencils are to our Patriarch, that (I know not on what account) represent him, both as to age and features, not becoming the foster father

of

of Jesus, and spouse of Mary. In all probability the Son of God would not provide a husband to his beloved Mother, who had the least personal defect; and although he might be forty when the blessed Virgin was fourteen, yet he ought not to be exposed, as leaning on a staff, and so decrepit as to be almost useless, when he was vigorous and able to work thirty years in serving the sacred family at home and abroad. S. Bernard is of opinion, that *S. Joseph was the likeness of Mary;* and the learned Gerson adds, that *the face of Jesus resembled the face of Joseph,* whom his royal progenitor David foretold would be the *most beautiful among the sons of men, Psal.* xliv. 31. conformable to the word of God, *a father is known by his son. Ecclef.* xi. 10. Joseph therefore had the agreeable features of Jesus and Mary; his very person was to create respect, reverence and affection, in the three eastern princes, who came to adore their Redeemer, and infant God, in obscure Bethlehem. He was not only consort, but constant companion

to

to the Queen of Heaven, and ſeeing that beauty, according to S. Auguſtin, is a gift of God, rendering his works amiable, the omnipotent Son, who had full power to qualify his Father upon earth, would not refuſe this additional ornament to his other diſtinguiſhing perfections. The Bethulian Judith was admired by Holofernes, and the whole camp of the Aſſyrians, God himſelf giving finiſhing ſtrokes (*Judith.* x. 4.) to compleat the lovely object; ſuch like favours granted to her and others, cannot in any equity of conſtruction be ſuppoſed refuſed to Joſeph. It may be verified of him more than of inconſtant *Iſrael thou art my ſervant, I will glory in thee. Iſaias* xlix. 3. His life was all of one piece, and not partycoloured. What relates to particulars will be briefly explicated afterwards by meditations, from the time of his joyful birth, to his moſt happy departure in the divine arms of Jeſus.

B   CHAP.

CHAP. II.—*At what Time the Devotion to* St. Joseph *became universal.*

THE great Alexander, standing before the tomb of Achilles, lamenting his own misfortune, and magnifying the advantage of the famed warrior: *Happy Achilles,* said he, *who had Homer to describe his conquests;* of which, notwithstanding, the greatest part is the product of poetical fancy. Let us extol the honour of S Joseph, and say, *Thrice happy he! who had the Omnipotent to be his panegyrist!* We have already heard how the Holy Ghost has derived his pedigree from Abraham; the Scriptures take notice of him, by name, whenever occasion presents itself; angelical messengers from heaven are several times (*S. Mat.* i. 20. *S. Mat.* ii. 13, 20.) dispatched to him, and commanded to address Joseph; the *Son of God was subject and obedient to him, Luke* ii. 51.; and had he been living when Christ bled on Mount Calvary for all mankind, questionless, he would have stood,

hero

hero like, with his dolorous spouse under the cross. Notwithstanding these encomiums, and what may be deduced from them, the brighter lustre of S. Joseph's glory did not dart its beam from the clouds till many ages after his departure. It is true, S. Chrysostom, S. Gregory Nazianzen, S. Peter Chrysologus, with other ancient writers here and there delivered in short sentences their sentiments concerning his merits and glory; but these may be termed rather transient hints, than intended panegyrics: for the devotion met not with any extraordinary encouragement till the reign of Pope Gregory XI. of that name, in the fourteenth century.

The first place P. Barrie knows of consecrated to his memory, is a chapel in the cathedral church of Avignon, dedicated to S. Agricola. The altarpiece represents the Patriarch conducting Jesus and Mary into Egypt. Round about this chapel this Pope placed his coat of arms, and large escutcheons of stone, encreasing at the same time the revenues of the Canons.

of that church. Perchance this was petitioning S. Joſeph to diſpoſe Italy for his reception, the Vicars of Chriſt having continued ſeventy years abſent from Rome, *de faƈto* he returned to his Roman chair five years after his creation, which was *anno* 1370. So it ſeems as if S. Joſeph (who brought our Lörd out of Egypt) was inſtrumental in Gregory's return, from a private city in France to the capital of the world. There belongs to the abovementioned chapel a confraternity of Bachelors, and a ſodality of Virgins, who in the ſolemn proceſſion on his feſtival carry in their hands poſies of flowers, as emblems of the fragrant odour of his eminent virtues. In our age devotion to him is univerſal through the habitable world : his feaſt is of precept, proper hymns are appointed in the divine office to ſing his praiſes and prerogatives, every one contending to be the foremoſt in his favour.

But *why?* (ſays the modern critic) *why* were the glorious merits of St. Joſeph ſo long concealed? *Why* not gene-

generally made known to Christians before the 14th century? True believers are to tremble at *why's* and *wherefore's* in divine government. It was the ensnaring *quære* of the envious and malicious serpent, which was the master-spring to ruin Adam and all his numerous posterity. *Why hath God commanded you not to eat? Gen.* iii. 1. A reason for the precept! It is unpardonable presumption to enter into the Omnipotent's hidden secrets, and damnable curiosity, to dive into his secret decrees: it is sufficient to have evidence, *God has commanded it, the Omnipotent and Omniscient has so ordered it, his ways are unsearchable, and who has been his counsellor? Ad. Roman.* 11. 33, 34. Infinite Wisdom knows best why universal devotion to the *keeper of his Lord*, is of so fresh a date. I offer something of the like nature by way of retortion, which carries no difficulty in the solution.

Moses having got a sight of the land of promise from the mountains of Nebo and Phasga, died in the land of Moab, and the Lord buried him in

B 3   - the

the valley of Moab, *and no man knows his sepulchre unto this present day. Deut.* xxxiv. 6. We know why he and Aaron were not permitted to enter the land of promise, but are absolutely ignorant, why God would bury him with private obsequies. *Why* would not the Creator, *glorifying them that glorify him,* 1 *Reg.* ii. 30. honour Moses (who spoke to *him face to face, Exod.* xxxiii. 11. *as man is accustomed to speak to his friend*) as much as an inferior prophet Elizeus, whose very bones in the sepulchre, by a casual touch, revived a dead body ? 4 *Reg.* xiii. 21. Again, the archangel Michael contended with the devil, concerning the body of the said Moses, *Epist. Jud. v.* 9. *why* this strife, *wherefore,* and to what end ? *When* was it ? What was the subject of the hot dispute ? The solid answer to this and other unknown resolves in divine administration, is that of St. Paul, *who on earth has been God's counsellor ?* however prudent and pious interpreters, with humility and submission, offer to return an answer
to

to the rash *why's.* The Hebrew nation was so stupenduously prone to
the horrid crime of idolatry, that even
when they were so terrified with divine Majesty thundering on the fiery
mountain, they petitioned that Moses
might *speak to them, not the Lord, lest
they died. Exod.* xx. 19. Yet a few
days after, concluding Moses to be
suffocated with the continual and
thick smoak, or to have been struck
dead by some thunderbolt, (*Abulens in
Exod.*) they prostrated themselves before a deformed idol, owning the
molten calf to have been their merciful deliverer from Egyptian slavery.
If therefore they impiously adored
what they knew to have been formed
out of their *wives, sons and daughters
ear-rings (Exod.* xxxii. 2.) and bod-
kins, what would they not have done
having certain possession of the *law-
giver's body?* of his who had wrought
so many prodigious wonders (they
were eye-witnesses of) both in E-
gypt and in the desert, both on land
and in the Erithean seas? it is much
to be feared they would have deified

the

the Thaumaturgus, as blind gentility placed Jupiter, Mars, and other renowned heroes in the number of the fictitious gods. To prevent so horrid an attempt, no *man knows the sepulchre of Moses unto this present day.*

This seems to answer sufficiently *why* the primitive ages took not full cognifance of St. Joseph's merits and glory, nor reprefented them clearly to Chrift's faithful. Becaufe Moles was fo great a man, therefore his body was concealed; and becaufe St. Joseph was fo fublime a faint, it feemed expedient to the Catholic Church, directed by the Holy Ghoft, not to appoint him any public honours. Obferve the reafon; fcarce was Chriftianity well fettled, when the Ebionites attempted to rob our bleffed Redeemer of his divinity, affirming moft facrilegioufly, that Jofeph was the natural father of Jefus; and by confequence, they denied the angelical virginity of the Mother of God. The preaching up at that time St. Jofeph's prerogatives, and eminent glory, would have given feeming encouragement to thofe
blaf-

blasphemous heretics, and likewise
might have stirred up dangerous
thoughts in weak believers. For men,
as is observed, are too frequently carried on to extremes, in honouring
such as they love and admire, and the
enlarging on what has been said already, with what wit and eloquence
could set forth in his praises, might
have suggested forcible doubts, that
possibly he was the natural father of
Jesus, because the real husband of
Mary; especially conversing with the
Ebionites, who were learned men of
affected sanctity, and agreeable behavi-
our. Therefore the Catholic Church
proceeded most prudently, chusing
the other extreme, and passing him o-
ver in long silence, while she celebrated the memory of many, who
could not pretend to stand in competition. These heterodox opinions,
having been detected, detested and
extinguished, the danger ceases, and
therefore universal devotion to the
Foster Father of Jesus is ferverously
entertained, and highly applauded,

where-

where-ever the Chriftian religion is profeffed.

The Omnipotent doth not order any thing but by the ftrict rules of fit difpofitions and fuitable preparations, in the exacteft meafure and weight, (*Sapient.* xi. 21.) proportioning particulars to time and circumftances, as to his infinite wifdom feems conducing to his greater glory. This fupreme Being, who fo frequently in the Old Teftament calls himfelf *the Lord of hofts, the God of armies,* is infinitely vigilant over his Church Militant up on earth, that the rebellious *gates of hell may not prevail,* St. Mat. xvi. 18. He feafonably fends forth frefh fupplies to oppofe diabolical adverfaries, and notorious fpreaders of erroneous doctrine: in the law of nature the holy patriarchs faced the enemy; in the written law commiffioned prophets fought valiantly in the front of his forces; in hours of grace, the apoftles and their fucceffors, lawfully fent, force back the approaching rebels. Even care is taken againft the confummation of the world; Enoch
and

and Elias are yet living as a reserve
to head the elect in opposing mon-
strous Anti-Christ in his violent ca-
reer; whose short reign will be attended with so great tyranny and ter-
ror, that *were it possible the very chosen
would conform and be led into error.
Mat.* xxiv. 24.

The protecting and sweet providence of God, from the very birth of
Christianity according to respective
necessity, has from time to time raised
up religious orders to curb and humble bold broachers of libertine novel-
ties, disagreeable and dishonourable
to the pure doctrine of Christ Jesus.
This Lord God of Armies has strength-
ened his Church in the last corrupt
ages, as some are piously of opinion,
by the conquering reserve St. Joseph
especially against those who craftily
lurk within the pale and offer the
rankest poison, in the golden cup of
reforming morals. To learned di-
vines, this appears an answer of no
small weight *why* the universal devotion was not entertained till the here-
tical contagion threatened a general

B 6   infection

infection in most provinces, and kingdoms, to the end the faithful might
more perceptibly and efficaciously experience the power and protection
of the Patriarch, calling on him with
greatest fervour (the devotion being
in its meridian) to defend *his* pure
doctrine, whose *divine person* he protected upon earth.

Other congruous reasons might be
alledged why this devotion is of a late
standing; but I hasten to shew how advantageous it is.

CHAP. III.—*Of the powerful Assistance
of* St. Joseph *to his devout Clients.*

THE illuminated St. Teresa of Jesus, celebrated for frequent re-
velations, and religious observance,
who successfully reformed the calced
Carmelites, and erected monasteries
and convents for both sexes, that she
might surmount such difficulties, which
to prudent men appeared insuperable,
took the glorious St. Joseph for her
lord and advocate, She honoured
him above all other saints, stiling him
her

her *father* and *master.* Under his auspicious protection, she a poor vir-gin, founded thirty-two religious houses, notwithstanding the opposition of secular princes, and several of her own order and profession. Take her own expression in commending this saint out of the sixth chapter of her Life, out of obedience penned by her-self.

"I have seen clearly that this Fa-
"ther and Lord of mine (St. Joseph)
"hath drawn me, as well out of this
"necessity (being crippled with sick-
"ness) as out of others greater, when
"there was question of honour and
"loss of my soul, and that with more
"benefit and advantage than even
"myself could tell how to desire.
"Nay, I cannot remember that hi-
"therto I ever desired any thing by
"his means which he hath failed to
"obtain for me, and it is able to a-
"maze me when I consider the great
"favours which Almighty God hath
"done me by means of this blessed
"saint, and the dangers both of soul
"and body out of which he hath de-
"livered

" livered me; in such sort that as it
" seems our Lord hath given the grace
" and power to other saints to suc-
" cour, in some kind the necessities
" of men; but I find, by good ex-
" perience, that this glorious saint
" succours us in them all; and that
" our Lord will make us under-
" stand, that as he would be sub-
" ject to Joseph upon earth, and that
" by enjoying the name of his father,
" and being, as it were, his director
" and tutor, he might then command
" him so; also now in heaven he
" would grant whatsoever this saint
" should desire.   This truth has been
" known by the experience of others,
" whom I have desired to recommend
" themselves to this saint, and now
" many are become devoted to him,
" and I myself have fresh experience
" of this truth.——Whosoever wants a
" master who may instruct him to
" pray, let him take this glorious saint
" for his guide, and he shall never
" lose his way."   Thus St. Teresa
declares her sentiments, and in several places of her excellent treatises,
the

she recounts how St. Joseph miraculously assisted her, not only in erecting monasteries, but also in dangers when travelling on such occasions.

St. Francis de Sales, that apostolical prelate, and deservedly prince of Geneva, was a signal promoter of devotion to St. Joseph. Founding the holy order of visitation, he put the first monastery under his protection; he ordered his feast to be kept with greatest solemnity in all their houses, directing by the institute all his spiritual children to make application to him; that the mistress of the novices should cause those upon trial, and even candidates, to get a habit of calling upon him when they begin their mental prayer, to take him for their guide and master in this holy exercise, respecting him as their tutelar patron.

St. Francis preached twice the same day at Lyons in honour to St. Joseph, as if he could never sufficiently enlarge in his praises. He also has left in writing his sentiments of this saint, in his Spiritual Entertainments, out of which I recite these few words:—

"O!

" O! what a great faint is the glori-
" ous St. Joſeph!—He is not only a
" patriarch, but the chief of the pa-
" triarchs; he is not only a confeſ-
" for, but more than a confeſſor; for
" in his prerogative of confeſſor is
" included the dignity of biſhops, the
" generoſity of martyrs, the purity of
" virgins, and the perfection of all
" other faints." The laſt clauſe of
this moſt illuſtrious biſhop, viz. he
having the perfection of all other
faints, affords ſtandard weight to what
was ſaid in the firſt chapter.

These two glorious faints, with ſeveral others before mentioned, erected publicly the ſtandard of St. Joſeph,
and ſuch as liſted themſelves experienced advantageous aſſiſtance. Probably St. Tereſa and St. Francis were
ſo eminent, and ſo far advanced in an
interior life, becauſe this patriarch
was their ſpiritual doctor. Hear the
former's opinion on this point: " I
" have not known any one, who is
" ſeriouſly devoted to this glorious
" faint (Joſeph), and performs to him
" ſeveral ſervices, whom I find not
" alſo

" alſo to be much advanced in vir-
" tue; for he aſſiſts thoſe ſouls much
" that recommend themſelves to him."
Invit. S. Tereſ. 1 *c.* 6.

It is very obſervable, that thoſe who
aſpire to be interior perſons profit in
his ſchool; they have God before
their eyes in all their actions, through
his interceſſion, who was near thirty
years in the continual preſence of the
Word Incarnate. The ſolid perfection of a ſoul conſiſts much in interi-
or and intenſe acts, directing each
particular to the final end, which is
God's glory, without mixture of ſor-
did temporal motives. When St.
Mary Magdalen Pazzi ſaw B. Aloy-
fius Gonzaga in glory, it was given
her to underſtand, that the reſplen-
dent crown was the reward of his frequent and ferverous interior Acts.
F. Severin, in a printed relation, recommends to poſterity what profici-
ents ſuch are who are under the di-
rection of St. Joſeph. He accident-
ally met a young man, and entering
with him into pious diſcourſes, diſco-
vered that he was highly enlightened,
and

and replenished with more than ordinary gifts. He gave himself to prayer and recollection, was weaned from all affection to creatures, and what the sottish blind world runs after greedily and admires. Although he was not trained up to much learning, yet he discoursed not only like a saint, but a solid divine. F. Severin proposed to him many questions, among the rest, if he was not devout to St. Joseph? To the last he replied, " For six years past he has been " my director and protector; our Sa- " viour himself assigned him for my " patron; next to the blessed Virgin " he is the greatest saint in heaven, " and had the plenitude of the Holy " Ghost, like the apostles."

For what regards the maladies of the mind, St. Joseph has found wonderful success. F. Barry instances several remarkable cures in love and hatred, two predominant passions, which frequently appear almost incurable, and also of despair and shame to comply with duty. A certain person was so desponding with doubts of per-
severing

severing in a religious state, that she was just upon the precipice of ruin, yet reciting nine days the beads of St. Joseph in his honour, she overcame the temptation she was sinking under. Others were wallowing in the sink of sensuality, and were immediately drawn out by this pattern of purity.

It is related of a lady, who was happily delivered from a deplorable slavery and miserable thraldom of mind, by the mediation of this saint, after the following manner:—Fear and shame had such an ascendant over duty, that obligation could not prevail with her to procure a performance of what conscience suggested absolutely necessary, viz. *A sincere confession of her sins.* To break through these difficulties, she had recourse to St. Joseph, reciting his hymn and prayer nine days; on the last, she was touched with deep remorse, and was assisted with sufficient courage to expose the gangreening ulcers, the holy patriarch smoothing the rough way to the confessional. In gratitude the

con-

convalefcent, or to fpeak more properly, the perfectly cured lady carried afterwards an image about her neck of the Fofter-Father of Jefus, to terrify the tempter for the future, from approaching her with any of his dangerous and damnable fuggeftions.

To fhew how tender St. Jofeph is of his clients, I relate a paffage out of Ifidorus. *(Lib.* 4. *c.* 10.*)* A gentleman of Venice, much devoted to the faint, was wont to recite daily upon his knees feveral prayers before St. Jofeph's picture. Being vifited by a mortal ficknefs, he had his thoughts more employed, as it frequently happens, concerning the recovery of his bodily health than the *one thing neceffary, (St. Luke* x. 42.*)* the fafety of his foul, and a happy departure from a fhort time to never ending eternity. St. Jofeph mindful of his paft fervices appeared to him, cautioning him to prepare for death, which drew nearer than was imagined. Hereupon he difpofed himfelf, begged the laft facraments, and had the

comfort

comfort of St. Jofeph's affiftance in his painful agony.

A gentleman at Paris, whofe character and habit, required an unfpotted life, had for five years abandoned himfelf to licentioufnefs, taking up the fordid practices of Epicure, and deferting the pure maxims of Jefus Chrift. Sound advice was loft upon him, and kind relations could not prevail with him to live at leaft in the world like a man of honor, as was expected from his quality. He ftill continued to poftpone the glory of his Creator, and fet a low value upon the joys of heaven. All was ineffectual; for he would not leave the crowd of unhappy tranfgreffors. Hereupon his friends having recourfe to higher powers, defired a Father of the Society of Jefus to celebrate holy Mafs in honor of St. Jofeph, and another of the fame body, not yet in holy orders, to offer up nine Communions, to the end the fcandalous delinquent might be ftopped in his notorious wicked ways. At the fame time their prayers were offered to God the party fell
moft

most grievously sick, and the indif-
disposition of his body was the cure
of his soul; for the violent distemper
increased to extremity, which so much
terrifyed him, seeing as it were by
serious reflections of what was past,
and what was to come, the very gates
of hell wide open to receive him, that
he reverently disposed himself, by the
Sacraments of the Church, to a Chri-
stian exit; resolving (if he recovered
his former state of health) to employ
his endeavours in a pious work of
great importance, and much conducing to God's glory. He recovered,
to the admiration of all and happily
compleated what he had purposed, to
the great edification and comfort of
such who knew any thing of his
former proceedings. He himself owned the power and goodness of St.
Joseph, in his sudden change and
perfect conversion.

A young man at Lyons, of distinc-
tion who had passed his years in the
fear of God, resolved to quit the
world, for the greater security of his
salvation, but was diverted from his
pious

pious refolution by friends and relations, acting out of temporal motives,
who like *animal men favoured not the
things that were from the Spirit of God,
for they are folly to them, and cannot
underftand it. (1 Cor.* ii. 14.) As
frequently we are *punifhed by what we
tranfgrefs in, (Sap.* xi. 17.) and tafte
the bitter *fruit of our own ways;
(Prov.* i. 32.) fo it befel thofe unkind
parents, diffuading the execution of
the heavenly call. The fon fruftrated
of his defigns and defires, and flight-
ing the former infpirations, began to
find an ebb of devotion, and from a
remiffnefs, there followed a total ne-
glect in fpiritual duties. He betook
himfelf to wars, and exercifed the
licentioufnefs of a profligate foldier,
not only letting loofe the bridle to
ungoverned paffions, but becoming
a noted ringleader to fuch as were
not afhamed to march after his black
ftandard. The afflicted father and
mother, too confcious of their miftaken affections, wept and lamented
without ceafing; they acknowledged
their error, in giving indirectly a beginning

ginning to unforefeen fcandals, they conjured him by frequent letters, to look back, they importuned by friends who refided near him, to have pity on his doleful parents, but all was in vain; his heart was depraved and hardened, his underftanding obfcured and befotted: in excefs of grief and confiding hope, they had recourfe to St. Jofeph, humbly petitioning him to ufe his meditation for bringing back the loft fheep, refolving to implore him daily, till he vouchfafed to hear their prayers. On the third day of their devotions, the prodigal fon returned home, caft himfelf in confufion at his parents feet; with fighs and tears he begged pardon for being the occafion of their long grief; he detefted his follies, reformed his life, correfponded with his former vocation, entered religion, and died in it exemplarily; this is another trophy of St. Jofeph's power and goodnefs.

The many votive pictures hanging round the altars of this glorious Saint proclaim fufficiently his univerfal protection. The number of his clients and

and miraculous cures would swell vo-
lumes; he not only lends an assisting
hand to distempers of the mind, but
likewise to the diseases of the body.
I give, in short a few examples, by
which a prudent judgment may be
framed, what passed in distant and
different parts of the world, and of
which P. Barry had no account or
knowledge.

Sister Jane de Angelis, was confined to her bed fourteen days, by a
formal pleurisy, which permitted her
not to rest day or night; she had been
let blood nine times in less than a
fortnight's space, and the quantity
taken from her occasioned such weakness, that she could scarce turn in
bed, none expecting any other change
but death, to free her from such torturing misery. She fell into violent
convulsions, like one ready to give
up the ghost, and though her exterior
senses did her little service, her judgment was clear and at full liberty.
' As I lay in this sad condidion' (hear
her own words) ' there appeared unto
' me a large and beautiful cloud, in

C   ' which

'which on my right side stood my
'good angel of incomparable beauty,
'like a youth of eighteen years of
'age, having in his right hand a fair
'wax flaming taper; on the other
'side in the cloud, was my holy father
'St. Joseph, with a countenance out-
'shining the sun in brightness, and a
'majesty more than human, resemb-
'ling in age, a man of forty or forty-
'five years.—Beholding me, he laid
'his hand upon that side where the
'principal source was of my distem-
'per, and anointed me with oil, or
'some such sort of liquid, and the
'anointed place remained something
'moist. At the same instant, I found
'myself perfectly recovered, and told
'the standers by as much.' Thus the
religious woman.

All with tears of joy magnified the
mercies of God, and the goodness of
the holy Patriarch, but Monsieur
Faveon, her Physician, and a Prote-
stant, was most astonished, when entering her chamber to visit this de-
spaired of patient, he found the family
upon their knees in prayer, which
                              made

made him conclude she was departed, but was immediately undeceived by the late agonizing woman herself, who arose from her knees, and walked towards him in her religious habit, with a smiling countenance recounted the particulars of her sudden recovery. He, who out-facing the best Historian and the holy Doctors of the Church, maintained miracles to have ceased, was forced to say *God is Omnipotent!* who gives visible marks of his true Church in these latter ages, as he was pleased to do at the first preaching of the gospel. This miraculous cure was fully attested by sworn witnesses, both as to her dying condition, and instantaneous resettlement in health, as appears by a long printed relation, approved by the most illustrious Bishop of Poictiers, wherein are several passages, here omitted for brevity.

This stupenduous favor was attended with two others of the like nature, eight days after. When Madam Laubougemont was seized with a desperate pleurisy, which four of the ablest

physicians

physicians of that place, judged incurable, and thought it in vain to apply remedies; she was then big with child which was a great addition to her dangerous circumstances, but understanding that the ointment, remaining on the side of sister Jane de Angelis, had been taken off with a fine linen cloath, and was carefully preserved, an express was dispatched in all haste to Loudun, desiring the favor of lending the cloth, which had wiped off the heavenly balsam. It was brought to the sick lady, and the odoriferous flavour filled her with sensible joy, application being made to her side, she found herself perfectly recovered. She was also freed from another danger, of almost equal hazard, being delivered a few hours after of a child, which the Doctors and Surgeons concluded had been dead a whole month in her body.

A strong young man at Laubougement, called Claud Murner, was brought so low and feeble by a violent fever, and an ulcerated swelling, extending itself from the ribs to the reins.

reins, that the Phyficians of Mafcon were of opinion, that the breaking of the ulcer would carry him off, or if he furvived the running of collected humours, he would remain a cripple all the days of his life. Upon this refult, fome of the fick man's relations advifed him to a vow to St. Jofeph, to confefs and communicate; a religious perfon offering the fame day, the unbloody facrifice, to implore St. Jofeph's Affiftance. This done, his fide being rubbed with what had touched the aforefaid linen cloth, and fwallowing a bit of paper, which had touched the fame, and upon which was written the moft facred name of Jefus, that very day the fever left him, the fwelling wafted away, his ftrength returned, fo that three or four days after he undertook on horfe-back a journey of feven leagues. What I have inftanced in thefe three perfons, happened to others at Lyons, Trevoux and Loudun, who by the fame means were cured of defperate diftempers.

Margaret Rigaud, a profeffed religious, in St. Elizabeth's Monaftery at
Lyons, fell from a floor one ftory high;
the bruife of her head was fo terrible,
that the blood gufhed out of her ears,
and deprived her almoft of fenfe. She
could not take any reft, even on the
fofteft pillow, and the evil increafing,
a confultation of Phyficians and Surgeons was held, who unanimoufly a-
greed the head was to be opened,
otherwife fhe would abfolutely lofe
her fenfes, if not her life. The languifhing patient defired the hazardous
operation might be deferred. In the
mean time her Superior moved by
divine infpiration, ordered a Com-
munion nine days together, in honor
of St. Jofeph for her recovery. The
violent pains continued eight days
without abatement, and the ninth was
running on, without any probable
appearance of a change; wherefore
fome of the religious propofed, that
the wounded creature fhould make a
vow to St. Antoline, who by her
interceffion, obtained relief in fuch
fort of bruifes and contufions. A fer-

vorus devotee of the holy Patriarch
being present, and unwilling that any
other should have the honor of the
cure, opposed vigorously the motion,
and begged their patience, at least till
the nine days were expired, which a
few hours would compleat. This being granted, she withdrew herself, and·
prostrating represented to St. Joseph
how the wounded and sick woman
had been first recommended to his
tender compassion, that he would not
permit any other to deprive him of
the glory, and seeing he had power
to relieve her, she conjured him by
the eminent prerogatives of being
nursing father to Jesus, and spouse to
the mother of God, to grant her re-
quest; promising a grateful acknowledgment to perform nine mortifica-
tions in his honor, and to recite nine
times his prayer, assigned by the holy
Church. Towards the close of the ninth
day, the sick person found herself so
perfectly cured, that rising up, she could
not contain herself from running
round the house, and proclaiming, *a
miracle, a miracle!* The glorious Saint

made

made her also happy, by an additional favor, viz. before her illness, it was a mortification to assist in the choir, and plain song seemed insupportable, but after the recovery, none was a more punctual observer of religious duties in the whole community: she set a high estimate on perfection, and chose St. Joseph for her principal Patron, for obtaining health to her body, but much more for divine grace to her soul.

The dreadful contagion of the plague is a visible scourge of God, it is a quick executioner of a provoked Deity, to make sinful nations sensible of the despised Omnipotent; it hurries on bold prevaricators by multitudes, to the inexorable judgment-seat, there to receive an unrepealable sentence according to the nature of their crimes. To prevail with the stubborn Hebrews for an observance of the written law, God declared by Moses that he would punish the infringers with a pestilence. *Levi.* xxvi. 25.) Which just threats are frequently repeated and inculcated, by the prophets

phets Jeremias and Ezekiel. For
David's vanity in numbering the people, the Almighty fent a plague upon
Ifrael, which fwept off feventy thou-
fand. (2 *Reg.* xxiv. 15.) And at the
full period of the world, mortals will
be punifhed with plague and famine.
(*St. Mat.* xxiv. 7.) It is needlefs to
give inftances of God's humbling
provinces and kingdoms in the Law
of Grace; it is yet frefh in memory,
how one of the flourifhing cities of
the world was laid wafte and defolate,
not half an age ago. The city of
Avignon was vifited by the plague,
near the beginning of the laft century. The inhabitants apprehended
utter defolation, made folemn vows
to God, in honor of St. Jofeph, to
obferve his feaft for ever afterwards
in the moft pious manner, which put
a ftop to the fpreading contagion.
This caufed feveral at Lyons, to have
recourfe to him in like dangerous
circumftances. Take the few following examples of the joyful fuccefs.

Monfieur Augery, an Advocate in
the Parliament of Dauphine, being at

Lyons

Lyons on the 15th of July, 1638, underftood that his fon Theodore, feven years of age, was feized by the plague, which as ufual occafioned a violent fever. A hard fwelling with the bubo, fhewed itfelf under the right arm. The afflicted father made a vow to God, that if St. Jofeph, by his interceffion, would procure his fon's recovery, and preferve the reft of the family, confifting of nine perfons, he would for nine days together vifit the Saint's Church, and bear fo many Maffes; he would offer wax candles at his altar, with a votive picture, as a lafting acknowledgment of the favor. In the mean time the fick youth was vifited by the Plague-furgeons, and although yet living, was given over and defpared of; accordingly, to prevent farther infection, he was carried to St. Lazarus's, the Peft-houfe; and that the miracle might appear more evident, at his arrival there he perfectly recovered, and not one of the family had afterwards the leaft fymptom of the diftemper. The father performed gratefully his promife,

hanging

hanging up at the Altar of St. Joseph a picture, movingly reprefenting his wife, children and himfelf on their knees, giving thanks to God for the favor obtained by St. Jofeph's interceffion. At the bottom, the miracle was exprelfed, and attefted by the Advocate's own hand.

Father Melchior de Faug, religious of the Society of Jefus, affifting thofe in the Peft-houfe to depart happily, was vifited by the fame infection, and lay in extremity, all defpairing his recovery. A Prieft of the fame order obferving him near expiring, made a vow (inviting the fick man to join with him) that upon the return of his health, he would offer nine Malfes for thankfgiving in the Church of St. Jofeph: at that inftant he recovered his fpeech, and likewife perfect health. The affiftance and protection of the moft holy Patriarch was fo manifeft, that thofe who were appointed mafters of health in Lyons, to attend the infected, recommending themfelves to St. Jofeph, were all preferved, although in the difcharge of

C 6　　　　　their

their charitable duty, they were daily exposed to evident danger. Wherefore after the plague was abated, in the year 1638, they came processionally in a body to St. Joseph's Church, there confessing, communicating and presenting offerings at his Altar, to express their tender gratitude for so signal a favor.

Tivenet, a pious old man, living near Lyons, in a village called St. Laurence D' Auger being infected with the plague, inquired of the Vicar of the place, who came to dispose him for eternal life, whether there remained any hopes of a recovery? No other, answered the Pastor, than to have recourse to St. Joseph, making a vow to solemnize his Feast yearly, and that day to confess and communicate, and for nine days to recite seven Pater's and Ave's concluding them with these words, Jesus, Maria, Joseph. The good old man made a vow, and that instant, found himself freed from the contagion, admiring what was become of the sores and swellings which so suddenly disappeared.　　　Bennet

Bennet Gontelle, a gardner, near St. Joseph's Church, lost every day one of his family consisting of seventeen persons; his wife and all his children had been carried to the Pesthouse, which was the next step to their graves; for there they died; he and a servant only survived, who expected hourly to follow the rest: Father Barry going to comfort them in that sad affliction, advised him to make a vow to St. Joseph, by which he should engage to offer several Masses and Communions in his honor if by his intercession he should obtain his, and his servant's preservation from the plague, which had so infected his whole house; and the good Father joined with him in the vow. Almighty God heard their prayers, and both were secured from the danger.

Martin de Bau, a child of four years of age, was struck with the infection on a sudden, whilst he was at play, and all gave him for lost. The affectionate mother being in great desolation, was counselled to recommend him to St. Joseph! *To you I recommend*

mend my child. Two hours after her hufband obferving figns of approaching death, called his wife, who made a fort of pious complaint in thefe few words, *Ah! St. Jofeph!* No fooner had fhe expreffed her grief in this manner, but the child recovered, called to his mother for meat, arofe from his bed, and cried out, *I am well, St. Jofeph hath cured me.* There remained not the leaft mark of his difeafe, and his ftrength was fo fully reftored, that the next morning he went to St. Jofeph's Church to return thanks. A votive picture was afterwards hung up, to teftify not only the child's, but likewife the father's delivery from the fame evil, by application to the bubo fome cotton that had touched the heavenly ointment at Loudun, wherewith St. Jofeph had cured miraculoufly a religious woman of that place, as is above mentioned.

I fhould pafs the bounds of this fhort treatife, were I to fet down the manifold favors granted by Almighty God at the interceffion of St. Jofeph. There is not any condition or ftate

of

of life, which has not experienced his power when invocated. Father Barry inftances this truth in virgins, married perfons and women travelling in child-birth. The devils in poffeffed perfons have frequently fhewn their indignation againft the Fofterfather of their Creator, and have trembled at St. Jofeph's name. St. Terefa faid much in few words, when acquainting the world as is fet down in the beginning of this chapter, 'that 'our Lord has given power to other 'Saints, to relieve us in fome particular neceffity, but that glorious 'St. Jofeph has power to fuccour us 'in them all.'

The holy Patriarch not only protects particular clients, but likewife whole communities and religious orders. Two centuries are paft, fince the never fufficiently praifed holy order of the Carthufians, apprehending a total diffolution, no fubjects offering themfelves to enter, held a general chapter at Grenoble: the main concern was to implore St. Jofeph's affiftance, in the dangerous condition

of

of their languifhing body, that it might not expire. To facilitate the way, and deferve compaffion from heaven, the congregated fathers chofe St. Jofeph as their patron and protector; they paffed an unalterable decree, that for the future his feaft fhould not only be obferved as of precept (which was not at that time commanded by the Church) but likewife that it fhould be folemnized, after the manner of one of the greateft days in the Roman Calendar. Thefe pious offerings were accepted by St. Jofeph, and proved fo efficacious, that in all parts of the world where they are eftablifhed, they have never fince wanted proper fubjects.

This glorious Saint brings alfo whole provinces and nations to the Catholic faith. New France owns him as a propagator of his gofpel, whofe legal parent he was. In the Southern parts of America, the chief Miffion is called, *the Miffion of St. Jofeph.* Under his aufpicious concurrence in the year 1626, two hundred families were baptized, and their

example

example influenced six neighbouring towns to unite themselves to the true faith, that they might partake of those spiritual and temporal blessings, which St. Joseph obtained for the thrice happy converts. From the entrance into that part of the world, the zealous missionaries had such an assurance of the Patriarch's power, that the fathers of the society gave the name of Joseph to the first Tarquois they baptized, offering him the first fruits of their apostolical labours.

What is already said, may be to Christ's faithful a sufficient proof of this comfortable truth, how those who are in St. Joseph's favor, have Jesus and Mary propitious on their side. The blessed Virgin encourages devotion to her beloved spouse and royal consort, witness that eminent master of spirit and prudent director of St. Teresa, Baltazar Alvares, S. J. who lying sick at Validolid in a burning fever, one of his order assisting him, held up an image of our blessed Lady and St. Joseph, advising him to recommend himself to the spouse of Mary;

Mary; ' You have reafon,' (faid Al-
varez) ' for the mother of God has
' commanded me exprefly to do fo;'
he owned afterwards that he received
this command in the holy houfe of
Loretto.   Favorites of heaven are not
only counfelled, but commanded to
practife and propagate devotion to
our Patriarch, as was clearly fignified
to St. Bridget and St. Gertrude. The
holy mother St. Terefa of Jefus, was
filled with infinite joy and delights
(to ufe her own words in the foundation of Avila) when on the feftival
of our bleffed Lady's Affumption, the
queen of all faints and angels, appeared to her with St. Jofeph; the
mother of God took her by the hand,
telling her that the fervice done to
her dear fpoufe St. Jofeph, pleafed
her very much, promifing affiftance
in her religious undertakings.   The
following chapter inftructs how we
may deferve to be taken notice of,
by the faid immaculate Virgin, by
honoring her beloved confort.

CHAP.

CHAP. IV.—*Divers methods of honoring St. Joseph.*

ISAAC, the fon of faithful Abraham, drawing near to his departure out of this world, ordered Efau to take his arms, his quiver and bow, *(Gen.* xxvii. 3.) to go abroad and provide by hunting, what might be agreeable to his aged father's palate, and fo receive *a blefsing before he died.* No man certainly can be fo grofly miftaken as to conclude from hence, that there was not variety at home to refrefh the decripid Patriarch. No, fays Lynanus, herein lies couched a myftery of morality, that a *fon who receives a blefsing muft be obfequious and ferve his father.* The paffage of the hiftory of the Eaftern Church, which was found and prefented as authentic to Pope Adrian the VIth. is highly comfortable; how our Lord Jefus Chrift affifting St. Jofeph on his death bed, leaned on his pillow, took him by the hand, received his laft breath, clofed his eyes, and immediately before this glorious parent
expired

expired, the Redeemer of all men gave him his bleffing for a happy paffage, with an affurance to beftow the fame on all thofe who fhould offer facrifice to God in honor of St. Jofeph, on the day of his happy departure, which the Roman Church celebrates on the nineteenth of March, the Greeks obferving it on the twenty fixth of December, as Baronius recounts in his martyrology. Though they differ about the time of his deceafe, yet they are unanimous as to the feftival of his efpoufals, viz. the twenty-fecond of January, of his flight into Egypt, on the twenty-fecond of December, and his return from thence on the feventeenth of January. In obferving thefe days, and performing other devotions to him, due regard is to be had to the above mentioned rule. *A fon who expects a bleffing muft be obfequious to his father.*

Works are more faithful declarers of the mind than words, or fole lip-worfhip. The crafty Gibeonites with greater fhew of eloquence and feeming piety, extolled the wonders of the Omnipotent,

Omnipotent, than favored Rahab as we read at large, in the second and ninth chapter of Josue. She said, *We have heard how the Lord dried up the waters of the Red-sea at your entrance, and what he hath done to the two Amorrhean kings Og and Sehon: But the men of Gibeon addressed Josue in the name of the Lord his God, proclaiming to the whole camp, We have heard the fame of his power, every thing he hath done in Egypt, and to the two kings on the other side of the river Jordan, Og and Basan, and Sehon of Hesebon:* what a glorious profession of divine power! this notwithstanding, the Gibeonites were condemned to perpetual slavery of drawing water and hewing wood, whilst Rahab was honourably entertained, taken in marriage by Salmon one of the chief princes of the Hebrew nation, from whose posterity our blessed Saviour Jesus was born. The solid reason of this different treatment was this; *Rahab believed with a firm faith, and with full devotion entertained the two men sent to view the land; Orig. hom.* 10.

in

in Josue) she acted as she believed ;
she ran the hazard of her life and
fortune in protecting the spies, and
setting them safe away; for had the king
of Jerico known that she concealed
them, no doubt herself and her house
would have been consumed to ashes,
before the Israelites set flame to the
city : whereas the pretended ambas-
sadors from Gibeon, calculated all
their projects according to the dissem-
bling rule of policy and self-preserva-
tion. Their contrivances and speeches
were ushered in by falsehood; and
although the Hebrew commander,
and the wise seniors of the Synagogue, were so far over-reached by
the fictitious narrative, as to swear to
a covenant, and spare their lives, yet
they were justly sentenced to drudge-
ry and slavery.

Wherefore it will be of little advantage to give fair words, and say,
*We have heard of the prerogatives,
power and protection of St. Joseph*; we
must perfect words by works, awake serious thoughts to serve God faithfully,
for this is the chief method of honouring

ing the Patriarch. It is pharifaical cant to cry, Lord! Lord! and ftop there; fuch hypocrites will not efcape the deluge of flames: and it ought to be remembered that the *olive branch*, brought by Noah's dove to the floating ark, prefaging peace to mankind, had not only *verdant leaves*, but was loaden with *fruit*. Hence a holy doctor of the Church gives neceffary advice, not to flourifh with *leaves only*, or *words*, but to *offer fruit*, *(St. Aug. Tract 6. in Joan.)* to entertain refolutely divine grace, to leave the tract of people out of the way, wandering towards eternal perdition, and by a virtuous life to deferve the favour of God, and the protection of St. Jofeph. But to defcend to more particulars.

If there is a feaft in the whole year (next to thofe dedicated to God, and the bleffed Virgin) giving affurance of obtaining our petitions and facilitating falvation, it is that of St. Jofeph. St. Terefa declares in the fixth chapter of her Life, " that for divers " years fhe defired fomething of him " upon

" upon his feſtival day, and ever found
" it granted; and if peradventure
" her petition was any way deficient,
" he redreſſed it for her greater good."
On that day holy ſacraments are to be
frequented, entertaining with flaming
devotion that Omnipotent committed
to the care of St. Joſeph. The votive oblation may be recited, and his
Life read over. It will alſo be a ſingular way of honouring him, if the
pious clients procure the ſacrament
of Holy Maſs to be offered to God in
thankſgiving for his eminent glory.

The univerſal practice of honouring our holy Patriarch, is to recite his
little office, his litanies, hymn and
prayer; either daily, or for a ſet time,
as occaſion or devotion require and
ſuggeſt. They are a compendious
eulogium of his praiſes. The following example will acquaint you how
acceptable they are unto him.

The Prioreſs of the Urſulins, of the
houſe of Coſe and Loudun, by Almighty God's permiſſion, was poſ-
ſeſſed with an evil ſpirit, who tor-
mented her after a violent manner.
To

To defend herself against his insulting tyranny, she was accustomed to crave St. Joseph's blessing (a devotion practised by many others) before the exorcisms, as a dutiful child would beg of a compassionate parent. She also obliged herself to recite daily St. Joseph's office, for a whole year, and to perform some weekly penance in his honour. Two or three days after the vow, the infernal enemy was forced away at the first exorcism, leaving the mark of a cross on her forehead, as the priest had injoined him; and to the end it might be known that it was at the Patriarch's intercession, the devil cried out hideously, *Joseph is come, and Leviathan must depart.*

Some religious of the said order of St. Ursula had a design to settle at Lambesa in Provence, the inhabitants testifying an earnest desire of their coming and company; wherefore they transported themselves thither, but met with unexpected difficulties and disappointments. They could not so much as find a proper house to hire, so resolved to return back to Aix,

from

from whence they came. In the mean
time they had recourfe to St. Jofeph,
they chofe him for the protector of their pious intentions, and refolved to recite after Mafs his Litany
for nine days together. Before the
ninth day, a virtuous prieft of fub-
ftance and authority came to difcourfe
the Urfulin fuperior: he had built a
church, and a houfe adjoining to it,
near Lambefa, in honour of St. Terefa: he made an offer to them both of
houfe and church, and actually put
them into poffeffion of both; as if
St. Terefa had directed him to provide for thofe devotees of her dear
father and *founder.*

A religious houfe of Nuns (as P.
Barry had from the mouth of a fuperior) had not received a confiderable
time any novices, which occafioned
great affliction, left in few years the
family fhould want fubjects to continue a fucceffion. They all refolved
to fay St. Jofeph's prayer after Mafs,
for fix months; which devotion being unanimoufly and cheaifully undertaken, that the Patriarch, who is
a pro-

a protector of religious orders, would vouchfafe to provide for them. A few days after a young lady of quality and fortune offered herfelf to live and die with them in God's fervice. The community was fenfible of the favour, and to this day continue their grateful acknowledgments. I cannot omit what is worthy of memory, the devotion of Monfieur Henry Chycot, canon of Chartres, which he expreffed for the aforefaid prayer. By his laft Will and Teftament, he left a confiderable fum of money, as a perpertual foundation, to be diftributed yearly amongft the canons of Chartres, with this obligation, to fing daily St. Jofeph's hymn and prayer; to the end he might contribute when abfent, in a more happy place, to have his fpecial patron honoured upon earth.

As moft perfons place in their beft rooms reprefentations in colours of fuch as they tenderly love, as teftimonies of their efteem and affection; fo the devout clients of St. Jofeph will do well to fet up his picture in their private oratories, or carry it in minia-

ture about them. St. Terefa practifed
this, and the little picture is ftill preferved at Avila. By our Lord's di-
rection, fhe placed over the gate of
her firft reformed monaftery, the fta-
tue of St. Jofeph, with that of his immaculate Spoufe. When St. Francis
de Sales departed moft happily at Lyons, there was but one loofe picture
found in his breviary, which was of
St. Jofeph. The aforefaid St. Terefa
now enjoys the lafting reward due to
her merits, and indefatigable labour,
in reforming an ancient religious order, and erecting thirty-two monafte-
ries. We by a perfonal reformation
of our lives, muft fit ourfelves for one of
thofe happy manfions in the houfe of
our heavenly Father, *St. John* xiv. 2.;
for a very fhort time will fix us in *the
houfe of our eternity. Ecclef.* xii. 5.
We muft not lofe fhort day-light in
carrying on the great work; but humbly beg St. Jofeph's helping hand,
that as he, father-like, affifted that
poor virgin in the reformation, fo
likewife he will favour us his peti-
tioners

tioners in taking secure possession of our glorious and everlasting mansions.

To prepare the way we are to make friends of Mammon, that when death calls upon us we may be received into *eternal tabernacles. St. Luke* xvi. 9. The prophet Daniel counselled impious and proud Nabuchodonozor, *to redeem his sins with alms-deeds, and his iniquities by shewing mercy to the poor, (Daniel* iv. 24.) : *per haps,* said he, *God will forgive* thy crimes, and mitigate the punishment. This is another method of deserving St. Joseph's favourable protection, to give alms to a man in years, to a poor woman and her infant, in honour of the sacred family of Nazareth. St. Vincent Ferrerius relates, how a gentleman of Valence had a pious custom, amongst his other good works, every Christmas-Day, to invite a woman with a sucking child, and an elderly man to dine with him, for the love he bore to Jesus, Mary and Joseph. This was so pleasing to God, that he had the comfort and joy to behold on his death-bed the divine

guests,

guefts, who were perfonated by thofe
he entertained; and as he was depart-
ing this world they gave him this
tranfporting invitation to paradife :—
" Friend, you have every year in-
" vited us to a feaft in your houfe,
" now come, and we will receive
" you to our feaft, and into the dwel-
" ling-place of the bleffed, there to
" reign with us, and them, in all forts
" of contentment, as long as a happy
" eternity fhall laft."—O! what comfort for fuch fmall matters, to *receive
a hundred fold, and eternal life. St.
Mat.* ix. 29.

St. Jofeph revealed himfelf, a devotion very acceptable to him, after the
following manner:—Two religious of
St. Francis's order having fuffered
fhipwreck, they happily laid hold of a
large plank, which bore them up; they
were toffed three days and three nights
in this evident danger of finking, and
in this ftarving diftrefs they had recourfe to St. Jofeph, petitioning his
powerful affiftance in their defperate
circumftances. The faint, though unknown, fhewed himfelf to them, like
a young

a young man of beautiful and comely features, he encouraged them not to despond, and, as a skilful pilot, conducted safe to a secure harbour. At their landing, they humbly craved the name of their deliverer, that they might personally acknowledge the singular favour? He told them his name was Joseph, and recommended to them the daily recital of seven *Our Father's,* and as many *Hail Mary's,* in memory of his seven griefs, and seven joys, which he related to them; and having said this, he disappeared. The good religious put the mentioned devotion into speedy execution, and likewise meditated on the mysteries suggested by him, who had secured them from the dangers of the deep. Peter Morales adds that St. Joseph had assured them, that he would succour others in necessity, and particularly at the hour of death, provided they practised the same devotion.

The holy Minim Gasper Bond had a laudable practice, at his going out of the convent, at his return, and in most of his actions, to call upon Jesus,

Mary

Mary and Joseph, that they would bestow a blessing upon his undertakings. On his death-bed he experienced incredible consolation, and begged of the assistants and visiters, that when they saw him agonizing, they would repeat with an audible voice these three sacred names. The last words he was heard to articulate on rendering of his soul to God, were, Jesus, Maria, Joseph. It is in the power of many to honour the name of Joseph, by giving it to children in holy baptism, or at the use of reason taking it in the sacrament of confirmation. Wicked sorcerers have been forced to own, that they have less power over infants that bear his name. It is a matter of fact, that a person of quality having lost all his children by withcraft, a few days after their birth, was counselled by one, who had too great an insight into that black and diabolical art, to name his next son Joseph; it was done, and the child lived to inherit his father's estate and honour.

The

The learned Gerfon obferves, how fuch who have loft any thing they much efteem, having recourfe to St. Jofeph, and performing fome devotions in his honour, either to retrieve what is gone, or bearing it with patience and refignation, are more favoured in fome other kind. He brings a proof of what he afferts, how an acquaintance of his recovered by thefe means what he had loft of great value. It is perhaps on this account that fcrupulous and anxious perfons, implore his affiftance, to obtain the ineftimable treafure of ferenity of mind, and interior repofe. He who experienced the lofs of Jefus, when remaining in the temple of Jerufalem, and the grief it coft him, doubtlefs will not be wanting to comfort his pious clients in anxiety and aridities. Not to pafs over in filence the merits of the above mentioned John Gerfon, know, that it is he who being the zealous and eminently learned Chancellor of the Univerfity of Paris, was fo paffionate a lover and admirer of our Patriarch, that he compofed a

D 5. book

book in his honour, intituled Jofephin ; and in all his eloquent fermons he never omitted to mention his praifes. He maintains, that he was fanctified in his mother's womb; that he had alfo abfolute command over fenfuality; that he was confirmed in grace; that he arofe with our bleffed Saviour Jefus Chrift; that, except the bleffed Virgin, no faint is greater in heaven. I could not omit this fhort digreffion, Gerfon having been felected as one of the chief panegyrifts of St. Jofeph.

Some, in refpect to St. Jofeph, invocate faints who bore his name, viz. St. Jofeph, fon to the Samaritan woman, that gave water to our bleffed Redeemer at the well of Jacob, (*Joan.* iv. 6.); his feaft is celebrated, according to Baronius's Martyrology, on the twentieth of March, fuffering then martyrdom with his mother and brother Victor. St. Jofeph the Juft, a title given him by the Holy Ghoft, *Acts* i. 23. He was one of the feventy-two difciples; and the apoftles had fo great an opinion of his fanctity,

ty, that they named him with St. Ma-
thias to be fubftituted in the traitor
Judas's apoftlefhip. The records of
Alexandria place him afterwards the
Bifhop of Jerufalem. The noble
Centurion, St. Jofeph of Arimathea,
feems to claim from Great Britain
particular veneration. This worthy
difciple of Chrift difcharged his duty
in time of greateft danger, when the
very Apoftles abfconded: at that time
animated by the dolorous Mother, he
entered boldly into Pilate's prefence,
not regarding his being cenfured an
enemy to the ftate, begged the body,
embalmed it, and had the honour to
depofite the fame in a fepulchre prepared for himfelf. He fupplied, as I
may fay, the place of our great Patriarch; the one providing for Jefus
living, the other took care of Jefus
dead upon the crofs, and for his interment. He came aftewards to preach
the gofpel in our ifland, and founded
our firft primitive monaftery of Glaf-
tenbury.

A religious man of Montferat ufed
to meditate frequently upon St. Jo-

feph's

feph's journey into Egypt, how he had afforded all manner of fervices to his God and to his chafte Spoufe. He intermixed repeated thanks to the princely Patriarch, for what he had done upon all occafions for his dear Redeemer, and the Virgin-Mother his fpecial advocate. It fo fell out, that on a time, being at fome diftance from his monaftery, and returning home, he miftook the road, and wandered up and down, and round a mountain, fo long, that he gave himfelf for loft; he was not without apprehenfions of a violent death from favage beafts, which often fhewed themfelves in that place, or perifhing by contagious fogs. The folitude of the night increafed the horror, and no means to efcape appeared, but to implore Heaven. He therefore recommended himfelf in the moft fervent manner to St. Jofeph's protection. No fooner had he done this, but he found the good effect of his prayer. He immediately met a grave man leading an afs, upon which fat a woman with an infant in her arms. This

happy

happy encounter was entertained with a wonderful comfort and joy, which was confiderably augmented, when afking the way, he who led the afs offered to be his guide, and bid him follow. As they went together, the whole difcourfe was of God, and the religious never found his affections fo charmed even in time of fervorous prayer. Entering the village, where the monaftery ftood, they all three difappeared, which gave affurance that St. Jofeph had delivered him from the danger; fo acceptable it was to meditate on fome paffage of his life, and to thank him for the care he took, and pains he underwent for him, whom we adore in heaven, and upon our altars.

There are feveral other ways of honouring him, as to fay the beads, to wear rings with his name engraved, as fome did at Lyons in the time of the peftilence, and not one of that number were touched with the contagion; others have on their rings, Jefus, Maria, Jofeph. But he is chiefly honoured, as is above faid, by honouring
God

God in the imitation of his virtues.
The pious reader may pick up what
is moſt proper for his ſtate. I mention one virtue, becauſe the bleſſed
Virgin was pleaſed to reveal to St.
Bridgit, that it had merited a particular crown of glory to St. Joſeph. It
was an uninterrupted ſeries of aƈts of
conformity to the Divine pleaſure. In
this he took ſo great ſatisfaƈtion, that
it was his frequent aſpiration, *Oh!*
that I may live to ſee the will of God
fulfilled. (In Revel St. Bridgit) Whether he ſaw his Saviour in the manger, or was obliged to withdraw into
Egypt, whatever happened, did not
contriſtate this juſt man, (*Prov.* xii.
21.) he never changed countenance,
but was equal in the inequality of human contingencies. We may without toil imitate the Patriarch, by de-
ſiring *only to live to fulfil the will of*
God. Neceſſary reſignation will make
us eaſy in all contrarieties and diſap-
pointments It is both diſpleaſing to
our Maker, and contrary to right rea-
ſon to fret and vex ourſelves at what
is not in our power to prevent. It
                                    alſo

also frequently happens, that what we lament as wanting is more beneficial than what we prayed to obtain. A true believer must walk towards everlasting bliss, betwixt prosperity and adversity, with a contempt of both. Such men as censure God's government of the world, are not only malecontents, but open rebels. Although they mutter and murmur, it makes no alteration in divine decrees, *for his counsel stands and his whole will is justified.* (*Isaias* xlvi. 10.) The Almighty is a most tender Father, and an unerring master, he takes care of *every hair of our heads,* (*Mat.* x. 30) and provides better for us than we could do for ourselves, bestowing temporal blessings or salutary scourges, according to what conduces to the improvement of his servants, who like royal David, *bless the Lord in all times, his praise is always in their mouths.* (*Psalm* xxxiii. 2.) Whether they are upon Mount Thabor or Mount Calvary, they would not change their posts, because God had placed them there. This perfect con-
conformity

formity goes hand in hand with conflant joy, *for in the throng of human miferies no mortal is more happy than he, who is what he would be. (Salvian. L. 1. de Provident.)* Such fouls as refolve ferioufly to enter after Chrift into glory, muft fuffer with him, and humbly beg to partake of his divine appointments, and never to abandon him, even when fweating blood in the garden, and praying to his heavenly *Father, not as I, but as thou wilt have it. (St. Mat.* xxvi. 39.)

Other particular virtues of St. Jofeph, may be taken notice of, in the eight meditations of his life; they need no orator to commend them, no more than a jewel of ineftimable value, a foil to fet it off.

Devotions to St. JOSEPH, *Spouse of the blessed* Virgin Mary. *With Meditations upon several passges of his Life.*

An Oblation to St. Joseph to choose him for a Patron.

O Holy Joseph! Virgin-spouse of the Virgin mother of God, most glorious advocate of all such as are in danger or in their last agony; and most faithful protector of all the servants of Mary your dearest spouse: I *N. N.* in the presence of Jesus and Mary, do from this moment choose you for my Lord and master, for my powerful patron and advocate, for the obtaining a most happy death: and I firmly resolve and purpose, never to forsake you; and never to say or do, nor even to suffer any under my charge to say or do, any thing against your honor; receive me therefore for your perpetual servant, and recommend me to the constant pro-
tetlion

tection of Mary your deareſt ſpouſe, and to the everlaſting mercies of Jeſus my Saviour: Aſſiſt me in all the actions of my whole life, all which I now offer to the greater and everlaſting glory of Jeſus and Mary, as well as to your own. Never therefore forſake me, and whatſoever grace you ſee moſt neceſſary and profitable to me, obtain it for me now, and at the hour of my death, to which I now invite you, againſt the uncertain hour in which it ſhall happen, that whatſoever at this preſent, and on my death-bed, I cannot of myſelf obtain, may by your gracious interceſſion be beſtowed upon me, by the God of my ſoul our Lord Jeſus Chriſt, who together with the Father, &c,

Ex Man. Tyrnavien.

THE OFFICE OF ST. JOSEPH.

At Mattins.

Jeſus, Mary, Joſeph.

V. O Lord open my lips.

R. And my mouth ſhall declare thy praiſe.

V. O

V. O God, incline unto my aid.

R. O Lord, make hafte to help me:

V. Glory be to the Father, and to the Son, and to the Holy Ghoft.

R. As it was in the beginning, is now, and ever fhall be, world without end. *Amen, Alleluiah.*

The Hymn.

JOSEPH, the fon of David was efteem'd
Father of Jefus, who the world re-
deem'd.
The Virgin he efpous'd,
In heart conjoin'd,
And Guardian was of both by heaven affign'd.

Ant. All hail honor of the Patri-archs, fteward of the holy Church of God, who didft conferve the bread of life, and the wheat of the elect.

V. O holy Jofeph, pray for us.

R. That we may be made worthy of the promifes of Chrift.

The Prayer.

ASSIST us, O Lord, we befeech thee, by the merits of the fpoufe of thy holy mother, that what of our-felves we cannot obtain, may be given

us

us through his interceffion. **Who**
liveft and reigneft with God the Father, in unity of the Holy Ghoft,
world without end. *Amen.*

At Prime.

Jefus, Mary, Jofeph.

V. **O** God incline unto my aid.
R. O Lord make hafte to
help me.

V. Glory be to the Father, &c.
Alleluiah.

The Hymn.

WHEN thou the Virgin with
child perceive,
Perplex'd in thought, thou her de-
fign'dft to leave.
But in thy fleep an angel with his
voice,
Advis'd thee not to fear, but to rejoice.

Ant. All hail honor of, &c. *as before,* p. 91.

The Prayer.

ASSIST us, O Lord, we befeech
thee, &c. *as before,* p. 91.

At

At the third Hour.

Jesus, Mary, Joseph.

V. O God incline unto my aid.
R. O Lord make haste to help me.

V. Glory be to the Father, &c. Alleluiah.

The Hymn.

TO Bethlehem, with the pregnant Virgin he,
Travel'd to pay th' imposed subsidy:
Where Christ was to be born, and in which place.
He shortly should his infant Lord embrace.

Ant. All Hail honor of, &c. *as before,* p. 91.

V. O holy Joseph, pray for us.

R. That we may be made worthy of the promises of Christ.

The Prayer.

ASSIST us, O Lord, we beseech thee, &c. *as before,* p. 91.

At the sixth Hour.

Jesus, Mary, Joseph.

V. O God incline unto my aid.
R. O Lord make haste to help me.

V. Glory

V. Glory be to the Father, &c.
Alleluiah.

The Hymn.

WHEN cruel Herod th' inno-
cents oppres'd,
By th' angel warn'd, thou call'dst thy
spouse from rest;
That taking her celestial babe, she
might,
With thee to Egypt, make speedy
flight.

Ant. All hail honor of the patriarchs, steward of the holy Church of
God, who didst conserve the bread of
life, and the wheat of the elect.

V. O holy Joseph, pray for us.

R. That we may be made worthy
of the promises of Christ.

The Prayer.

ASSIST us, O Lord, we beseech
thee, &c. *as before*, p. 91.

At the Ninth Hour.

Jesus, Mary, Joseph,

V. O God incline unto my aid.

R. O Lord make haste to
help me.

V. Glory be to the Father, &c.
Alleluiah.

The Hymn.

THY foes being dead, thou mad'ft
no longer ftay ;
But into Galilee didft bring away,
Mother and child, heaven this advice
did give,
And thou at Nazareth did'ft humble
live.

Ant. All hail, honor of, &c. *as be-fore*, page 91.

V. Pray for us, O holy Jofeph.

R. That we may be made worthy
of the promifes of Chrift.

The Prayer.

ASSIST us, O Lord, we befeech
thee, &c. *as before*, p. 91.

At Even-Song.

Jefus, Mary, Jofeph.

V. O God incline unto my aid,
R. O Lord make hafte to
help me,
V. Glory be to the Father, &c.
Alleluiah.

The Hymn.

BLESS'D Jefus (of thine eyes the
glorious light)
At twelve years old was loft, unto
thy fight.   But

But finding him among the doctors thou

His guardian was, to whom the angels bow.

Ant. All hail honor of, &c. *as before*, page 91.

V. Pray for us, O holy Joseph.

R. That we may be made worthy of the promises of Christ.

The Prayer.

ASSIST us, O Lord, we beseech thee, &c. *as before*, page 91.

At Complin.

Jesus, Mary, Joseph.

V. CONVERT us, O God, our Saviour.

R. And turn away thine anger from us.

V. O God, incline unto my aid.

R. O Lord, make haste to help me.

V. Glory be to the Father, &c. Alleluiah.

The Hymn.

O Happy man, to be embraced by Christ and the Virgin in death's agony:

That

That so thou might'st thy course di-
    rectly bend,

To Limbo, having made a godly
    end.

Ant. All hail, honor of, &c. *as before,* page 91.

    V. O holy Joseph, pray for us.

    R. That we may be made worthy
of the promises of Christ.

The Prayer.

A SSIST us, O Lord, we beseech
    thee, &c. *as before,* page 91.

The Commendation.

T HESE hours canonical I have
    addres'd,

To thee St. Joseph from a zealous
    breast :

That by thy prayers, thou wilt obtain
    that I

May live with thee, in heaven eter-
    nally, *Amen.*

THE LITANY OF ST. JOSEPH.

L ORD have mercy on us.
    Christ have mercy on us.
Lord have mercy on us.

Christ

Chrift bear us.

Chrift gracioufly hear us.

O God the Father, Creator of the world, have mercy on us.

O God the Son, Redeemer of mankind, have mercy on us.

O God the Holy Ghoft, perfecter of the elect, have mercy on us.

O facred Trinity, three Perfons and one God, have mercy on us.

Holy Mary, Queen of the whole World,

St. Jofeph, Spoufe of the bleffed Virgin,

St. Jofeph, fanctified before birth,

St. Jofeph, privileged and preferved from all mortal fin.

St. Jofeph, confirmed in grace,

St. Jofeph, Honor of the Patriachs,

St. Jofeph, replenifhed with unfpeakable benedictions,

St. Jofeph, reputed Father of Jefus,

St. Jofeph, abounding with all the gifts of the Holy Ghoft.

St. Jofeph, who adored Jefus in the crib,

St. Jofeph, an Angelical Man,

Pray for us.

St.

St. Joseph, who by the admonition of the good Angel preservedst Christ from the fury of Herod,

St. Joseph, who (as a principality of the first Hierarchy of Angels) didst govern Christ·

St. Joseph, who as a virtue, wert minister to Christ,

St. Joseph, greater than the Dominations, whom the King and Queen of Heaven obeyed,

St. Joseph, in whose arms and bosom Christ was seated as in a throne,

St. Joseph, who as a Cherubim, hadst care of the Virgin of the true Paradise,

St. Joseph, a seraphical Man,

St. Joseph, a most high contemplative soul,

St. Joseph, who diedst in Christ's arms,

St. Joseph, who didst hear angelical music,

St. Joseph, Precursor of Christ to the holy Fathers in Limbo.

St. Joseph, who arose with Christ from the dead,

Pray for us.

E 2

St.

St. Joseph, who in body and mind, did enjoy peculiar gifts of glory,

St. Joseph, our dear Patron and Defender,

Lamb of God, that takeſt away the ſins of the world, ſpare us, O Lord.

Lamb of God, that takeſt away the ſins of the world, hear us, O Lord.

Lamb of God, that takeſt away the ſins of the world, have mercy upon us.

O Lord, hear my prayer:

And let my ſupplication come to thee.

The Prayer.

ASSIST us, O Lord, we beſeech thee, *as before,* page 91.

The Hymn in honor of St. Joseph.

HAIL holy Joſeph, whoſe pure mind,

Render thee fit to be deſign'd,

The huſband of a moſt pure bride,

To royal David both ally'd.

Hail guardian of God's Son on earth,

Foretold of his ſtupendous birth,

And other heavenly secrets known
But to thyself and spouse alone.
   How often did thy happy arms,
Secure that sacred babe from harms:
When with him, and thy Virgin-wife,
Constrain'd to fly, to save his life!
With what unspeakable delight,
Didst thou enjoy the precious sight!
Of thy Redeemer whose bright eyes,
Did far out-shine the sun's uprise.
   How many times didst thou em-
     brace?
The tender giver of all grace,
And didst as often fix a kiss,
To fill the measure of thy bliss?
   To whom did God such joys im-
     part,
As to thine own and spouse's heart?
Which did strange comforts entertain,
When Jesus lost, was found again.
Most happy was thy house, to be
The Paradise, in which the Tree
Of Life did prosper, when the ground,
Where that first grew, could not be
     found,
How sweetned was thy daily pains,
While Jesus lived on thy gains!
Whereby the food that ye did eat,
Became all sanctified meat.

With thee he frequently did walk,
Calling thee father in his talk;
And by his charming sweet discourse,
Did sorrows from thy heart divorce.
No instruments, however strung,
'Ere sounded like our Saviour's tongue;
Which thou heard'st hourly! happy
    then,
Wert thou above the rest of men.
    And when in age, resistless death
Gave summons to thy latest breath,
Cou'd thou more happiness devise,
Than to have Jesus close thine eyes.
Great is thy glory sure above,
Whom Christ did so entirely love,
As on thy person to bestow,
Such privileges here below.
Then let us all, with one consent,
Beseech Saint Joseph to present,
Our wants to God; and for us pray,
That serve our Lord we ever may.
    Amen.

The Prayer.

OMnipotent and merciful Lord
    Jesus, who didst provide Saint
Joseph, the just son of David, for
spouse of blessed Mary, thy Virgin-
mother, and chose him for thy nurs-
            ing

ing Father: grant, we befeech thee, that by his prayers and merits, thy Church may enjoy a perfect peace, and fo arrive at the confolation of thy everlafting vifion. Through the fame Lord Jefus our Saviour, who with the Father and the Holy Ghoft, liveth and reigneth one God, for ever and ever. *Amen.*

THE BEADS OF ST. JOSEPH.

UPON the great beads, you recite the following prayer which the holy Church makes ufe of in his divine Office.

The Prayer.

ASSIST us, O Lord, we befeech thee, by the merits of the fpoufe of thy moft holy mother, that what of ourfelves we cannot obtain, may be given us by his interceffion: Who liveft and reigneft with God the Father, in the unity of the Holy Ghoft, world without end. *Amen.*

Upon the leffer Beads you fay,

MOST glorious patriarch St. Jofeph, fofter father of Jefus, and fpoufe of the ever immaculate mother

of

of God, pray for us now, and at the hour of our death. *Amen.*

———————➤

Seven Prayers in honor of the Seven Dolours and Seven Joys of St. Joseph.

The first Dolour.

The tormenting thoughts of forsaking his spouse with child.

The first Joy.

The comfortable message of the angel, *Joseph, son of David, do not fear to take Mary for thy wife.*

The Prayer.

O Chaste Joseph! I most humbly petition by this grief and this joy, that you will make supplication for my being preserved in unalterable purity of soul and body, that I may overcome all temptations and perplexities, curb my censuring others, and that I may, by concurring with divine inspirations, deserve the favourable assistance of my good angel, in directing me to the performance of my duty towards God and man, through our Lord Jesus Christ, who with the Father and the Holy Ghost,

liveth

liveth and reigneth one God, world without end. *Amen.*

Our Father, &c. Hail Mary, &c.

The second Dolour.

St. Joseph's beholding little Jesus shivering with cold in the manger, and so miserably accommodated.

The second Joy.

His hearing the angelical harmony. The adorations of the shepherds, and the three kings prostrate before the Infant God.

The Prayer.

COmpassionate St. Joseph, I most humbly petition, by this grief and this joy, that you will make intercession for me, that my frozen heart may become a fervent receptacle of my dear Redeemer in the adorable Sacrament of the Altar; and my poor soul a permanent dwelling-place of the Holy Ghost. I now freely offer my memory, will and understanding to be governed by divine providence, beseeching God by your merits, that I may adore him so faithfully on earth, as to deserve to sing eternally with the blessed angels,

that

that joyful canticle, Glory be to God on high, through our Lord Jesus Christ.

Our Father. Hail Mary.

The third Dolour.

St. Joseph's beholding Christ to shed his sacred blood so early in the circumcision.

The third Joy.

His pronouncing the most sacred and saving name of Jesus, as the eternal Father had ordered by the angel.

The Prayer.

SAINT Joseph my potent patron! I most humbly petition by this grief and by this joy, that you will make intercession for me, that I may shed tears of perfect contrition, for being the occasion of my dear Redeemer's shedding his most precious blood; that if called to a trial for his sake, I may chearfully offer up my life to him who gave it. I also rejoice that my Jesus was pleased to bleed at that tender age, to ransom me and all mankind from everlasting perdition. I likewise beg that the saving name of Jesus may be so deeply imprinted in my my heart and memory, as never to think, say, or do any thing against God's honor, through the same Lord Jesus Christ, &c.

Our Father. Hail Mary.

The fourth Dolour.

The words of Simeon on the day of the purification, *that a sword should pierce the blessed Virgin's heart.*

The fourth Joy.

What Simeon said, that Christ would be a light to the Gentiles, the glory of Israel, and resurrection of many.

The Prayer.

SAINT Joseph! comforter of the afflicted, I most humbly petition by this grief and this joy, that I may be tender and compassionate in the sorrows and misfortunes of my neighbour, that I may partake fully of the dolours and merits of the blessed Virgin, standing under the heavy cross of her bleeding Son, to the end my Saviour may be a clear light to me in walking the narrow way by a holy life, towards the beatifical vision of my God, and a glorious resurrection,

E 6   Though

Through the same Lord Jesus Christ,
&c.

Our Father. Hail Mary.
The fifth Dolour.
Christ's flight into Egypt, occasioned
by persecuting Herod.
The fifth Joy.
The falling down of Egyptian idols,
at the approach of the Son of God.
The Prayer.

HOLY St. Joseph! perfectly re-
signed to Almighty God's fatherly appointments and permissions;
I most humbly petition by this grief
and this joy, that I may willingly
submit and carefully conform to whatever crosses or contrarieties, the divine wisdom and infinite goodnefs fee
expedient for me, that I may be as
equally thankful in the sharpest adversity, as in flourishing prosperity. That
I may by your intercession experience
the unspeakable joy of trampling on
and keeping under foot the deformed
idols of inordinate passions, and vain
sordid pleasures, so much courted and
adored by the vicious world, through
our Lord Jesus Christ, &c.
Our Father. Hail Mary.

The sixth Dolour.

The fear St. Joseph had at his coming from Egypt, hearing that Archelaus reigned.

The sixth Joy.

Orders from heaven by an angel, to return home with Jesus and his blessed mother.

The Prayer.

VIGILANT St. Joseph! careful guardian of Jesus and Mary, look down from heaven upon a poor client surrounded with many dangers of falling into sin, and dropping into hell, I most humbly petition by this grief and this joy, that you will intercede for me, that I may not fear any thing but offending my good God. Protect me from the tyranny of infernal powers, and beg by the passion of Christ, that he will compassionate my infirmity, and enable me with his grace to walk cautiously betwixt love and fear, through the dangerous Egypt of this uncertain life, so as to enter joyfully the blessed land of promise, to enjoy never ending happiness, through our Lord Jesus Christ.

Our Father. Hail Mary.

The seventh Dolour.

St. Joseph's looking for Jesus at twelve years of age, when returning from Jerusalem.

The seventh Joy.

His finding Jesus in the temple, sitting among the Doctors, who were astonished at his wisdom.

The Prayer.

SAINT Joseph, my powerful Advocate, who in the losing and finding of Jesus, experienced the two extremes of intense anguish and transporting joy; I your unworthy supplicant most humbly petition, that I may never lose my God by mortal sin, although it were to enjoy as many pleasant worlds as Omnipotency can create. I now seriously repent and will lament, during the remainder of my life, for having so frequently parted unconcerned with divine grace. I having nothing worthy of acceptance to atone for my crimes and pay off my debt. I offer the merits of my Redeemer, which he has made my own, and you glorious Foster-father of Jesus, offer for me all the aforesaid Dolours

'lours and Joys, that by worthy fruits of penance I may feek my Creator forrowing, and after a happy death, adore him in the heavenly Jerufalem, there to enjoy what the heart of man has not conceived, through our Lord Jefus Chrift, &c.

Our Father, &c. Hail Mary, &c.

Eight MEDITATIONS upon fome paffages of the Life of St. JOSEPH, which may ferve through his Octave, or at other times.

MEDITATION I.

Of the Sanctification, Birth and Name of Jofeph.

The Preparatory Prayer.
Beg humbly of God, that your memory, underftanding and will, may be employed to his greater honour and glory, in this mental prayer.

Firft

First Prelude.

Imagine yourself at Nazareth, at the birth of St. Joseph, and ponder the difference wherewith men and blessed spirits regarded this Royal Infant.

Second Prelude.

Beg light to see the vanity of the world, and grace to despite it.

POINT I.

Consider. THAT St. Joseph was sanctified in his mother's womb. *Gerson, Serm. de nativit. Virg. habita in Concilio Constantiens. Et. 3. Part. Alphabet. 59. lib. 2. Officium Hierosolomit. Jacobus de Valentia super Magnificat*, being designed for a higher ~~station then~~ that of St. John Baptist, or the prophet Jeremy, who both were saints before their birth. Admire and love the purity of this holy infant. His soul was more charming by sanctified grace, than all the celebrated faces of the world. We may truly say, O beautiful St. Joseph! many rejoiced in your nativity, both angels and expecting souls in limbo, you being born, who

who was to be the legal father to the long promifed Meffias, fpoufe to the Mother of God, governor of Jefus, and mafter of the facred family, you appeared like a clear dawning of the day, ufhering in the glorious fun of juftice. · I congratulate with you for your early fanctification, and I give thanks' to my God for the prerogative defigned you from all eternity. I take complacency that you are raifed fo high above other faints, and it will be a fatisfaction if fo infignificant a creature as myfelf can any ways promote your honour.

POINT II.

Confider. THIS noble infant was born in a poor little houfe, without fuch diftinguifhing marks of grandeur as are never wanting at the birth of princes. Reflect, that as *the heavens are far exalted above the earth, fo are the thoughts of God different from thofe of men.* Ifaias 55. Rebelling worms of the earth fit under the fhade of triumphant laurels, although as vicious as bloody
Nero

Nero and savage Dioclesian, whilst Job the Idumean prince is scorned upon the dunghill, and Joseph the next heir to the sceptre of David is not taken notice of. After this man-ner the Almighty treats his chosen favourites. The *poor* rich man, who was cloathed in silks, and purple, who feasted splendidly every day (St. Luke 16.) sitting under a stately canopy, and adored by his flattering parasites, was so intoxicated with pride that he doated on his own misery: in that mistaken flourishing state, he was odi-ous to his Creator, contemptible to the angels, and notwithstanding his funeral pomp the Son of God wrote his dreadful epitaph, *burned in hell!* whilst the *rich* poor man fainting at his gate, for want of the cast-away crumbs, and consoled by dogs licking his ulcers, was waited on by angels, to take his place among patriarchs, prophets, and kings. O the beauty and riches of holy poverty! O the dangerous circumstances of those who receive more temporal favours than others, which will render their

judg-

judgment more terrible for abused
bounties. Lord open my eyes to see
and contemn the frothy pomp of the
world. Give me a found judgment
to undervalue myself. Create a clean
heart in me, removing that which hitherto has been hardened, by the interceffion of St. Joseph; correct my
tepid and stupid thoughts, that I may
pity and pray for unfortunate mortals,
who look not forward to confider
what it is to *be buried in hell,* from
whence there is no redemption or return.

POINT III.

Confider. THE fignification of the
name of Joseph, viz.
increafe. No fooner did he attain
the ufe of perfect reafon than he was
inflamed with the love of God, and
feeing St. Mary Magdalen de Pazzi,
made a vow of perpetual virginity at
ten years of age, probably our angelical patriarch offered this ineftimable
treafure at a more early hour. He
increafed fo ferveroufly in all manner
of other heroic virtues, as to deferve

after-

afterwards the second throne (as many doctors are of opinion) of all saved souls in heaven. Most holy God! I blush and am confounded in your pure presence, looking back on the black sins of my depraved youth. I own to have abused the first rays of reason, in turning into the broad way of the world: my first lessons were to study my satisfaction, to be esteemed, and I ran mad after the erring multitude. As I increased in years my crimes increased; now being sensible of all worldly folly, I penitently return. Receive me at the eleventh hour, you, who had compassion on the good thief, when ready to expire upon the cross.

The Colloquy.

BLESSED St. Joseph, sanctified in your mother's womb, and born to the joy of men and angels, make powerful intercession for me, that my pious resolutions may not prove abortive; that I may be born to an interior and spiritual life; that I may have such an increase of sanctity, such an ardent love for purity, such abject

thoughts

thoughts of my own vilenefs, fo clear a light to view worldly greatnefs which is *vanity of vanities*, as to undervalue all things which deferve not the character of true wifdom and heavenly virtue, through our Lord Jefus Chrift.

MEDITATION II.

Of the humble Calling of St. Joseph.

The preparatory prayer as in the former meditation.

Firft Prelude.

Imagine yourfelf at Nazareth, beholding St. Jofeph a comely youth, exercifing the laborious trade of a carpenter.

Second Prelude.

Beg of Almighty God to inftruct you how in your prefent ftate of life you may attain true perfection.

POINT I.

Confider. HOW divine Providence ordered that St. Jofeph of royal extraction fhould be trained up

up in the humble exercife of a carpenter. 1. Not only for his perfonal
maintenance, but that this contemptible calling might balance the future
dignities that were to be conferred
upon him, and to refemble the humble
life of the Meffias. 2. That he might
decline idlenefs, fo dangerous to his
vowed chaftity. 3. That he might be
a pattern to men living in the world,
how they might be much in God's
favour. 4. That by the labour of his
hands he might be enabled to beftow
the nobleft charity in fupporting the
Son of God and his immaculate Mother. My foul! upon all occafions
rejoice in divine appointments, and
take full notice that folid perfection
is not confined to the folitary cells of
Nitria. An unregarded artifan has
taken place in glory of all the rigid
Anchorets. Whoever ferves his God
more faithfully, and loves him more
ferveroufly, than the filent reclufe,
will have a more refplendent crown.
Rejoice that your Creator encourages
and entertains impartially all his fervants according to their merit, by co-
operation

operation with his grace, congratulate
with St. Joseph for being so great a
favourite of heaven. Take a strict
account of yourself how time is employed from morning to evening,
ponder what is amiss, and resolve upon regulation, by the intercession of
St. Joseph.

POINT II.

Consider. THAT amongst other motives determining St.
Joseph to exercise this calling was the
love of humility and mortification.
He had so clear a knowledge of God's
greatness, that he thought he could
not descend too low. O my soul!
what different ideas have you of divine Majesty and divine Justice?
You neither love your Creator as a
father, nor fear your Redeemer as a
judge. St. Joseph had little to satisfy
for, but he would offer acts of supere-
rogation, whilst I stand upon terms
with God, stopping at strict obligation; and alas! too often transgress
against indispensable commandments.
Reflect likewise on the false notion

of

of worldlings concerning mortification; who conclude, that voluntary
sufferings appertain to such who have
renounced the world, and live in convents, as if the sinner deserved not
greater punishment than the saint.
Ponder how often you have heinously
injured God, whilst perhaps the mor-
tified religious never lost baptismal
grace. Take up the cross in time,
mortify yourself to satisfy for past
trespasses. Be liberal to God if you
expect extraordinary lights and im-
pulses. Be careful, by a guard over
the senses, to preserve a pure interiour.
Beg, by St. Joseph's intercession, that
you may not displease God venially,
even by the cast of an eye or a dis-
edifying jest.

POINT III.

Consider. HOW St. Joseph's painful life was accompa-
nied with purity of intention, directing all his thoughts and words, performing all his actions to the greater
glory of God. This practice prepared him for the prerogatives, dis-
tinguishing

tinguiſhing him from other mortals. A right intention entitles to reward what in itſelf is indifferent, as being not commanded nor prohibited: it gives ſtandard weight to the meaneſt of our actions, it advances a treaſure to attend us at taking leave of the world, and is a ſort of continual prayer. Lament the irrecoverable loſs of many actions, not being meritorious, for the defect of pure intention. You never wanted vain and malicious intentions, obeying the ſuggeſtions of the infernal enemy. Deſert him for the future, and whether you eat, drink, or ſleep, make an offering, and tell Almighty God you comply with theſe neceſſities to pleaſe him. Take St. Joſeph for your maſter, to teach you how to join exteriour employments with interiour intention and attention.

The Colloquy.

OMnipotent Creator! whoſe unerring providence adds joy every moment to the angels in heaven, and to ſaints upon earth, I moſt humbly beg by the interceſſion of St. Jo-

F　　　　　　ſeph,

feph, that I may chearfully acquiefce
and rejoice in every thing that comes
from your fatherly hand. That I may
be vigorous in executing your divine
will, and glorify you in my prefent
ftate. Grant me the true fpirit of
mortification, to fubdue my ftubborn
paffions, to fatisfy for what is paft, and
to be a prefervative from future dangers. Grant, that by purity of intention the meaneft of my actions
may be acceptable to you, as the two
little mites were of the poor widow,
thrown into the treafury of the temple. Through our Lord Jefus Chrift,
&c.

MEDITATION III.

Of the Marriage of St. Jofeph.

The preparatory prayer as in the
firft meditation.
Firft Prelude.
Imagine yourfelf to be in the temple of Jerufalem, when the high-prieft
gave to Jofeph the immaculate Vir-

gin Mary. How the patriarch espoused her, by putting a ring upon her finger, with other ceremonies according to the written law, in token that he made her partaker of all his goods, and took her into his protection.

Second Prelude.

Beg light to understand the mysteries of this matrimony, and grace to reap fruit from hence.

POINT I.

Confider, THOSE words of Solomon, *Houfe and riches are given by parents, but properly a prudent wife is given by our Lord.* Prov. xix. 14. This feat of wifdom was fo great a blefling to St. Joseph, that he might truly fay, *all good things came with her.* Sap. vii. 11. She brought a plentiful portion for his improving in all manner of virtues. Chrift aflifted perfonally at the marriage in *Cana of Galilee,* and we may contemplate what a blefling was beftowed on a mutual contract of her who was to become the *Mother of*

God, and him whom the second Person of the Blessed Trinity was to obey. This was the most honourable marriage (*ad Heb.* xiii.) since the creation, and with a copious infusion of divine grace *God joined them,* St. Mat. xix. 16. Ponder likewise how the merits of St. Joseph promoted him to this dignity, *For a good spouse is given a man for his good actions,* Ecclef. xxvi. 3. Study to please your Creator, by purity of intention, in chusing a state of life. Endeavour to be much in God's favour by good works. If you have faith to remove mountains, it avails nothing without charity. The devils believe and tremble; they made a profession that Christ was the *Son of God,* (St. Mat. viii.) yet remained damned spirits. Such as live not up to their belief, have *the faith of devils, not of apostles,* St. Aug. Serm. 38. de temp. Lament the sins and scandals of your former life. Resolve for the future, by the intercession of St. Joseph, that both God and man shall see your good works, *and glorify the Father in heaven.* Consider

der alfo, that if it is your choice to
live in a married ftate, you ought to
cherifh your confort, to preferve peace
and union, to avoid contention and
mifunderftandings. As you make one
civil body, like the primitive Chrfti-
ans, have *one heart and one foul.* Love
your fpoufe as *Chrift loved his church,*
(Ephef. v.) who for the love of it laid
down his precious life. Beg bleffings
to your concerns by the interceffion
of St. Jofeph.

POINT II.

Confider, ALmighty God was pleafed to acquaint the world
in thefe two noble perfons, with the
dignity of virginity, and value of
vows. They both had confecrated
their virginity to their Creator, and
one was chofen to be the Mother, the
other legal father to the Son of God.
O ineftimable treafure of chaftity,
that renders mortal men like to angels. Unfpotted virgins fing canti-
cles before the throne of God peculiar to themfelves. Apoc. xiv. 3.
They attend the *omnipotent Son of God*
F 3 *wherever*

wherever he goes. The religious of both sexes, who profess and observe this evangelical counsel, may be called sons and daughters of Mary and Joseph. O virgin Mother, O virgin Spouse! beg and obtain for me chaste dispositions and desires. Ask yourself, whether edification and modesty appear in your conversation; if not, reform. Detest the company of such persons who even indirectly cast out words tending to levity. Fling aside or rather burn books which recount the successes of passionate love in creatures. Irregular suggestions pass from the memory to the understanding, and so to the will; remove the fuel to prevent the fire. Lament failings of what kind soever against this angelical virtue.

POINT III.

Consider, ST. Joseph provided for the blessed Virgin, and took her into his protection. Do you also promote her honour with those under your charge. Suffer not any one to speak with disrepect of her, or her

her glorious fpoufe. Avoid the converfation of thofe who leffen devotion to thefe great fouls. Have a filial confidence in their protection, and congratulate with yourfelf for being fo happy as to be devoted to them. Refolve to practife fomething to the honour of both. Do not be fo grofsly miftaken as to think eternal happinefs muft coft you nothing. Strip yourfelf of former fancies, and loathe what you hitherto have admired. Look up towards heaven, begin to overcome what you vainly feared: he is ftronger who ftretches out his hands to fave you, than he that keeps you back in thraldom.

The Colloquy.

OMnipotent God! at whofe command every tree produced *fruit in its kind* (Gen. i. 11.), grant me, by the interceffion of this noble Virgin-pair, that I may ferve you faithfully in the ftation you have placed me. I firmly believe every tittle you have revealed, yet help my incredulity, leaft I be in the unfortunate number of foolifh virgins who carried

lamps

lamps *without oil.* Assist me with your powerful grace, that I may act as I profess; that I may be humble, charitable and chaste, and not stand like the barren fig-tree, and be fuel for eternal flames; through the infinite merits of Jesus my Saviour. *Amen.*

MEDITATION IV.

Of St. Joseph's Journey with the blessed Virgin to visit St. Elizabeth.

The preparatory prayer as in the former meditations.

First Prelude.

Imagine yourself accompanying the blessed Virgin and St. Joseph over craggy mountains, to a place distant far off from Nazareth. Hearken to their discourse in this winter journey, and consider what was said in the house of Zachary. Reflect on St. Joseph's perplexity at his return home.

Second Prelude.

Beg grace to be charitable to your neighbour, to shun detraction and rash judg-

judgment, and to be devoted to the blessed Virgin.

Point I.

Consider, HOW some months after St. Joseph's espousal, and a few days after the angel had declared to the blessed Virgin the mystery of the incarnation, and likewise that her cousin St. Elizabeth was six months gone with child, she humbly desired leave of St. Joseph to visit her; but he out of his tender affection would not suffer her to go, without his personal taking care of her in that journey. O admirable charity! O profound humility! take hold of all opportunities of comforting and succouring your neighbour. If you move in a higher sphere above others, reflect, that to whom much is given much will be required of him. Condescend to inferiors: the Mother of God, prevented by a visit, the Mother of the Precursor. Who is the blessed Virgin, and who am I? My pride is inexcusable. O my soul! study to be dead to all vanities, to beware of dia-

E 5. bolical

bolical illufions, fuggefting fuch and fuch practices, become men of honour. Lord give me your holy love, and I am happy enough to pity wicked mo-narchs, even the moft flourifhing ones of the univerfe.

POINT II.

Confider, THE many bleffings that came by Mary. At her firft falutation St. John was fanctified, he leaped for joy in his mother's womb. St. Elizabeth was replenifh-ed with the Holy Ghoft, and prophe-fied, magnifying her maternity, cal-ling her the *Bleffed of women,* ad-miring her ftupenduous humility, that being *Mother of the Lord* fhe fhould come to her. O my tepid foul! learn to exult with joy at the receiv-ing of thy Saviour in the holy eucha-rift; make due preparations, by a fe-rious and fincere confeffion, humbly beg that the interceffion of Mary may be a means to procure thy fanctifica-tion, for by her God diftributes his favours Reprefent to her thy necef-fities, and beg an alms of her. Re-flect

flect also that if such wonders happened at the first hearing the voice of the blessed Virgin, to what a degree of sanctity must St. Joseph arrive, who conversed with her thirty years? If she obtains favours for notorious sinners, that by her prayers they return to the friendship of God, and are beautified with sanctifying grace, it is beyond our reach to comprehend what a fund of all virtues she procured for her dear St. Joseph. Contemplate how happy was the man *who had a good spouse* (Ecclef. xxvi. 1.), surpassing the excellency of the highest feraphim, and what a proficient he was in all perfection by her daily presence and heavenly discourse.

POINT III.

Consider, HOW the sublime virtue of St. Joseph was tried, when after his stay at Zachary's house, at his return home, he understood that his immaculate spouse was with child. What sharp conflicts passed then betwixt a pure conscience and chaste affections? He put the

moft

most favourable construction upon the occasion of his torturing affliction. He called to mind and revolved her unparalleled modesty and chastity, therefore would proceed cautiously, and not act with severity. He knew the long promised Messias was to be born of a Virgin, and why might not she be that happy creature? Learn to excuse the seeming faults of others, and if an unbecoming action shews several faces, look upon the least deformed; excuse the intention, conclude it accidental, and fear you would have done worse in the like circumstances. Bewail all rashness in censuring your neighbour. Ponder also St. Joseph's zeal for the law of God, which he infinitely preferred, as the chief object of his love, above whatsoever was under heaven. My soul! despise what is transitory, standing in competition with divine precept, prefer not again the villain Barrabas before thy God. Yet the Patriarch resolved to *dismiss her privately,* that she might not suffer in her reputation, and be stoned as an adultress. Be

you

you tender and compassionate in the failings of others; although they are matter of fact, prevent the spreading of them, give a check to such discourses. Consider likewise how the divine goodness afforded comfort when human means gave no relief. An angel is dispatched to acquaint him with the mystery. Oh what transcendant joy after piercing grief! Learn to expect the divine pleasure with settled resignation. Trust in the goodness of your God, accuse yourself of former diffidence. Congratulate with the blessed Virgin and St. Joseph for their mutual joy.

The Colloquy.

HOLY Ghost! my God of all comfort! if you see it expedient, for the greater security of my salvation, that I be tossed with tribulation, permit me not to sink. Infinite Power! bear me up, you know my weakness. Favour me with such graces, that I may be compassionate towards my neighbour, governing myself by the spirit of lenity and charity, as if the case were my own. I deplore

plore my cenforious temper, and I refolve to ftand upon my guard.   It is
a mercy you have let me fee my wick-
ednefs, I render you thanks for the
defires of becoming better, and for
not being worfe than I am; but becaufe of myfelf I am no more able to
keep a good purpofe than to remove
a mountain, I beg your affiftance that
I may fulfil what you command, and
then command what you pleafe. Af-
flict me with fuch croffes as I can bear,
to the end I may pay off the great ar-
rear due to divine juftice.   Grant me
by the interceffion of St. Jofeph, that
after my temporal trials, whether exterior or interior, I may find that permanent joy with which you render
his immaculate fpoufe, and him, eternally happy. *Amen.*

MEDITATION V.

*Of St. Jofeph's Virtues exercifed at the
Birth, Circumcifion and Prefentation
of Jefus in the Temple.*

The preparatory prayer as in the
former meditation.   *Firft*

First Prelude.

Imagine yourfelf with the bleffed Virgin and St. Jofeph in a ruinous ftable at Bethlehem, where Chrift was born, and laid in a manger betwixt an ox and an afs. How afterwards St. Jofeph circumcifed him, and gave him the holy name of Jefus. Laftly, how he prefented the Son of God in the temple, where he was met by Simeon and Anna.

Second Prelude.

Beg grace to profit by St. Jofeph's contemplations in thefe myfteries.

POINT I.

Confider, HOW St. Jofeph being returned from Zachary's houfe, was obliged to undertake a winter journey, to be enrolled at Bethlehem with his fpoufe, in compliance to Auguftus Cæfar's edict. He chearfully obeyed, fo ought you to do towards thofe who have command over you, even in difficult matters. What pious difcourfes had he on the road for thirty miles with his virgin fpoufe; he patiently endured the inconveniencies

encies in travelling, but many more at finding no place in the inn, and being forced to take shelter with an ox and an ass in a poor stable, to herd with brutes. How often have you entertained our Lord in the like manner, he entering a breast full of brutish passions, admire the patience of your Redeemer in suffering you to receive him so unworthily. The blind man knowing the king is present, stands with great respect, although he sees him not: you know that the Son of God visits you personally, yet remain stupid, as a senseless animal. Give frequent thanks to God that you have not been punished like Oza (2 *Reg.* 6.) who was struck dead for rashness in touching only the ark of the covenant, whereas perhaps you have more than once received the Lord your God most sacrilegiously. Reflect on St. Joseph's sorrow, seeing the vileness of the place, no accommodation, at midnight, in a rigid season. The Son of God would be born in these severe circumstances, he chose what he loved. Be ye vile in your own

eyes,

eyes, cut off superfluities by mortification. Beg that violent passions may freeze, that you may be a dwelling-place for Christ. The blessed Virgin and St. Joseph being rapt in prayer and contemplation, *the immortal Son of God* was born according to the flesh. He wept upon the cold ground, and St. Joseph joined with him tears of fatherly tenderness; at every infant-cry, he sent heart-breaking sighs to heaven, and prostrate before him, honoured him with heroical acts of faith like his, who said afterwards, *Thou art Christ the Son of the living God.* He adored his Saviour, he thanked him for his immense goodness. Imitate you these and the like acts. Lament that your sins were the occasion of our Lord's weeping in the manger. Reflect what joy succeeded, when the crib resembled paradise. Choirs of angels sang *Glory to their God,* the shepherds adored, the three kings in an humble posture offered rich presents to their almighty Sovereign. Do you also join with the heavenly spirits, rendering thanks for innumerable
ble

ble favours, which you may call to mind one by one. Offer your memory, underftanding and will to him who gave you them. Beg by St. Jofeph's interceffion, that you may adore God upon earth with an undefiled confcience, and eternally in heaven in glory.

POINT II.

Confider, ST. Jofeph's obedience to the law, in circumcifing his Saviour, who was exempt from it, yet would bear the badge of original fin though incapable of committing any. You excufe yourfelf criminally from fulfilling of the divine law, and ftudy to appear a faint, whilft you are an inveterate finner, examine, repent, deteft pride the fource of all evils. Jefus's humility confounds your haughtinefs. Refleft how St. Jofeph's heart was wounded with grief, before he faw the blood of Chrift; at pronouncing the name of Jefus he fell upon his knees, the nine choirs of angels proftrated, and all hell trembled, that name being to confound

their

their infulting over captive fouls. Offer tears of compunction to him, who
redeemed you with ftreams of blood.
Take not the name of the Lord your
God in vain, which is *holy and terrible*, nor fuffer any under your command to fpeak the language of devils.
As far as lies in your power concur to
the falvation of others. Since God
defcended from heaven to fave finful
mankind, do you condefcend to what
may be inftrumental in fo glorious a
work.

POINT III.

Confider, WHAT St. Luke records, *cap.* 2. *His
father* (fo the evangelift ftiles St. Jofeph) *and mother were marvelling at
what was faid of him.* They were in
extafies, hearing the prophecies of
Simeon and Anna. They marvelled
that *God fo loved the world, as to give
his only begotten Son.* They admired
the infinite goodnefs of Chrift con-
templating in him the boundlefs and
bottomlefs ocean, as it were, become
a drop, and the whole fiery fphere a
little fpark. They were aftonifhed

that

that he who created the univerfe with a few *fiats*, was to be redeemed with a pair of turtles. They offered him to the eternal Father, and to compleat this ineftimable purchafe, gave what was required by the law of Mofes. My poor foul! join with them in admiration, marvel that Chrift fhould love you, an ungrateful worm, fo ardently, as to weep for you, to bleed for you. Admire his divine patience in not punifhing your manifold crimes, whereas many have been cut off in the flower of their youth, and fent to burn eternally in hell, for fins far lefs in number than yours. Stand confounded, reproach yourfelf, for having fo frequently fold your Lord, like treacherous Judas, for petty intereft or fordid paflions; rejoice that he has ranfomed you, and gives you grace to purchafe his favour by leading a new life, refembling the fimplicity of the dove.

The Colloquy.

O My infant God! how truly may it be faid of me, *the ox has known his owner, and the afs the man-*

ger

ger of his lord, (*Isa.* 81.) but I have not known you. I admire your love and charity, I admire my tepidity and stupidity. Early goodness, I come too late to love you. Although at the eleventh hour, bestow on me the promised penny, be to me a Jesus, and you who both fed me, and bled for my misfortunes, let me partake of the universal charity. Grant by the intercession of St. Joseph, that my purposes may be perfected by vigorous execution. I also beg that when I entertain you in the most blessed sacrament, I may be favoured with such affections of adoration, love and thanksgiving, as St. Joseph experienced when he took you back into his arms from Simeon, to restore you to your blessed Mother. *Amen.*

MEDI.

MEDITATION VI.

Of the flight into Egypt, his Return from thence, and of the losing of Je-sus, and finding him in the temple.

The preparatory prayer as in the former meditations.

First Prelude.

Imagine yourself travelling with that blessed company, in so tedious a journey, and a rigid season, Jesus not being *one year* old *(Maldonatus in Matth. & alii)*, reflect how they spent their time for several years, at Helio-polis, which is interpreted the *City of the Sun.* How after their return to Palestine, they went to adore in Je-rusalem, where Jesus was lost, and found in the temple, sitting amongst the doctors.

Second Prelude.

Beg light, and grace to practise such virtues as St. Joseph exercised both in Egypt and Judea.

POINT I.

Confider, WHEN St. Joseph received the command, *Arife, take the child and his mother, and fly into Egypt,* he obeyed that very moment. He quitted home, country, conveniencies, to live amongſt perverſe idolaters, who hated the Hebrews. He travelled through deſerts, wanting ſometimes neceſſaries, paſſing from mountain to valley, to find a little ſpring to refreſh the fainting family. The love of Jeſus made all things eaſy to him. O my diſobedient ſoul! how often has God commanded me by *clear* infpirations, *arife,* perform that act of virtue, *fly* that dangerous company, burn that pernicious book, make háſte to the throne of mercy by ſerious repentance, and I ſlumbered on in my habitual tepidity, and ſlept in my iniquities? I will now *arife* with the *prodigal ſon,* I will make haſte to my heavenly Father, loving him, grieving and confounding myſelf, and purpoſing newneſs of life, and ſurmounting with divine grace all
.difficulties

difficulties laid in the way, by men or
devils. Ponder how it pierced St.
Joseph's heart, to see his God offended by thofe prophane idolaters. You
have fo little compaffion for other
finners, that you will not drop one
tear for your own crimes. St. Jofeph
took pleafure to be defpifed as a vile
artifan, working to fupport the facred
family. Your daily ftudy is to be
efteemed, you court vanity, and fhun
folid glory. My foul! bear up in
hard ufage, difown utterly the maxims of the world. Refufe not to be
cloathed with contempt, like thy Lord
and Mafter. Be not terrified with
an imaginary enemy, and league with
a real one.

POINT II.

Confider, THE ftedfaft hope, and
invincible fortitude of
St. Jofeph. His whole truft was in
divine Providence. He gave no attention to diabolical fuggeftions, viz.
Why to fly? Why fo far off? Why
at this feafon? Why into Egypt?
Why not to the three kings? who
would

would take it as an honour to entertain us, but to a perverfe nation,
where we cannot expect any other
treatment than affronts and ill ufage.
The holy Patriarch was deaf to this
language, he chearfully arofe at midnight, like the great Abraham, when
commanded to facrifice his fon Ifaac;
nothing could deter him to move one
ftep out of the road God had pointed
for him. All the monfters of Egypt
were looked on with difdain and contempt; *God was his hope.* Be not
you curious to pry into the divine
conduct, reject carnal arguments, diffuading from what the Almighty com-
mands. Fix your eye on heaven, and
as difficulties fhew themfelves, let your
hope encreafe. Beg by the interceffion of St. Jofeph, courage and refolution to quit all that is valuable upon
earth, rather than difobey the voice
of your Creator. Make reflext acts,
that the *All-powerful is your hope,*
who will fend relief in due time, as he
did to St. Jofeph by an angel, ordering the return of the facred family
back again to Paleftine.

G POINT

Po**i**nt III.

Consider, THAT every man was obliged to go and worship God, in the temple of Jerusalem, on the feast of Azims. It lasted seven days, and although St. Joseph might have made only his appearance, to fulfil the law, and return to Nazareth, yet he remained the seven days, taking that opportunity to satisfy his devotion by honouring the eternal Father in his own house. Endeavour you likewise to have interiour fervour and recollection, as well as exteriour reverence and modesty, at the time of divine service, and in private prayer. St. Joseph was apprehensive in coming back to Jewry, because Archelaus reigned there: now he fears not to appear in Jerusalem, where a cruel prince sat upon the throne, because the worship of God was concerned. Be you courageous in discharging your duty, despise human respects, and what the wicked world may say of you, by obeying God more than man. Consider also how Christ being lost,

St:

St. Joseph fought him with a forrow-
ful heart; he could not find him a-
mongft *his kindred and acquaintance,*
nor in any other place but the temple. If ever you be fo unfortunate
as to lofe our Lord by fin, lament bit-
terly, have recourfe to prayer, turn
from creatures, do not defpond, avoid
all occafions of relapfing, frequent the
holy facraments; for he is to be found
in the temple. Reflect on the two-
fold joy St. Joseph experienced at the
fight of Jefus; the firft, becaufe he
had found the God of his heart,
whofe profound wifdom was admired
by the moft learned doctors; the fecond, in hearing the bleffed Virgin
term him Jefus's Father, which prerogative was entertained with humility
and confufion, as thinking himfelf unworthy of that glorious title. St. Jofeph fought no efteem nor praifes;
that is my folly. I run after empty
fhadows of vanity, and decline real
glory! My foul! glory in the crofs
of thy Lord Jefus Chrift, and caufe all
the angels to rejoice at the return of
the loft fheep, *that is,* thy felf.

The

The Colloquy.

JESUS, my Maker and Master! without whose merciful assistance I walk in darkness, and perish, I most humbly beg through the intercession of St. Joseph, that you will teach me the direct road from my Egyptian slavery, the servitude of sin, under which I have so long groaned, to the liberty of your faithful servants. I have frequently experienced your goodness, and I know your power; my trust is in both. O! grant me constancy to contemn the allurements of the world, and to stand undaunted at afflicting terrors. My dear Redeemer! I have too often lost you by sin, I have willingly and wilfully parted with you, for what I blush to think on. Pity the unfortunate, you who come to seek sinners, of whom I have been the ring-leader. You are now pleased to bless me with so true a sense of my former trespasses, that I grieve not so much for the fear of punishment, as for that my sins have offended you, the circle and centre of all goodnefs. I ftedfaftly purpofe by thy holy grace to feek you ferioufly by the reformation of my life, that I may find you in the heavenly Jerufalem, reigning with the Father and the Holy Ghoft, world without end. *Amen.*

MEDITATION VII.

Of St. Joseph's many Years Converfation with Jefus and Mary at Nazareth.

The preparatory prayer as in the former meditation.

Firft Prelude.

Imagine yourfelf to have had the happinefs and honour of frequently entering the little houfe of Nazareth; and contemplate what probably was faid or done by the facred family.

Second Prelude,

Beg light and grace to practife virtue, in imitation of St. Jofeph, during the courfe of your whole life.

POINT I.

Confider, THOSE words of the
royal prophet, *with a
faint, you will become a faint,* Pfal.
xvii. 26. and contemplate how great
a proficient in fanctity St. Jofeph
muft have been by a daily and hourly
converfation for thirty years, with the
Holy of Holies, the *Son of God.* What
he learned in Jefus's fchool, is not
underftood by the moft elevated contemplatives. St. Paul, *rapt into paradife,* (2 Cor. xii. 4') *heard words not
lawful for a man to utter.* St. Jofeph
was made partaker of more divine
fecrets: and if the faid apoftle humbly gloried that *God made him a fit mi-
nifter of the New Teftament,* 2 Cor.
iii. 6. it cannot be conceived how St.
Jofeph was qualified to difcharge his
duty as legal Father to the Word incarnate, and real fpoufe to the Mother
of God. The long recollection of
Paphnutius, and the mental prayers
of Pacomius, are but rough draughts
of our holy Patriarch's uninterrupted
union with his Redeemer. He had

theological, cardinal, and other virtues in perfection under so great a
master. Consider each apart, and sin-
gle out something for imitation. Beg
of St. Joseph, by the merits of Christ,
and the love he bore to his immaculate Spouse, that he will be your
intercessor and instructor towards
learning the science of saints, reflect
on St. Joseph's care and pains to support the family; all labour was sweet
and easy because undertaken for Jesus
and Mary. If you have charge over
others, promote God's honour, and
permit not that he be offended: For,
*whoever has not care of those under
him, especially domestics, has denied the
faith, and is worse than an infidel.*
1 *Tim.* v. 8. If you connive at others
sin, you make them your own, and
although silent, you become an ac-
complice. Assist others in spiritual
or temporal necessities, and you employ your time like St. Joseph working to please Jesus.

POINT II.

Consider, THE words of Solomon,
Prov. vi. 27. *Can any*

man hide fire in his bosom, and his garment not to burn? Could St. Joseph have the infant God in his arms so close to his heart, and not burn with divine love like the highest Seraphim? When the two disciples travelled towards Emmaus, and our blessed Saviour risen from the sepulchre, discoursed them upon the road, they found their *hearts burning within them, whilst he spoke to them in the way. (St. Luke* xxiv.) St. Joseph was thrice happy in such discourse for many years, the Son of God declared to him the interpretation of the scriptures, and necessity of suffering. When Christ fell upon his knees to pray, Joseph and Mary by his side, the Patriarch lost himself in extasies, he annihilated himself in the presence of God; how often did he tell him, my Lord! you know I love you, joy of my heart, God of my soul! whilst tears of devotion came trickling down his face. Samuel mistook the voice of God, and took it for Heli's. Joseph had certainty in hearing the sweet voice of Christ, discoursing personlly personally with him. O my soul! prepare the way for divine grace by fervent prayer, and according to your station, set others on fire with the love of God and their neighbour. Defer not the time of your devotions, as if you designed to serve your Creator in the last place, let him have preference to insignificant conversation, and trifling visits; ponder also, that probably according to the rules of perfection, St. Joseph distributed the hours of the day. Some he set out for prayer, some for pious conferences, others for work, and so the rest according to exigencies; observe you likewise order, give good example, which influences more than words. Mistake not the voice of the enemy transforming himself into an angel of light. Follow the instructions of a prudent director, who will inform you what is suggested by hell and self-love.

POINT III.

Consider, **H**OW hard a matter it is, to find the true eleva-

tion of this refplendent ftar, St. Jofeph. If bright rays darted out from
Mofes's face, after forty days and
forty nights converfation with God on
Mount Sinai (or as fome doctors are
of opinion, with an angel deputed by
the Creator) infomuch that the princes of the Synagogue, durft not draw
near him, and the Law-giver placed a
veil over his face, *Exod.* xxxiv. 33.
What a glorious interiour had St.
Jofeph, who converfed with God
made man, face to face thirty years?
St. Paul in his defence agaiuft the
obftinate Jews, inftanced how he was
taught the law, at the feet of Gamaliel,
Acts xxii. 2. St. Jofeph learned the
higheft perfection of the law from
him, who delivered it to Mofes. In
his daily actions he united the active
and contemplative life, fometimes
working for Jefus, at other times fit-
ting at the feet of Jefus, and hearing
the word. He ftood aftonifhed to
behold him, who commanded the
world out of nothing with a few
words, working at the carpenters
trade, and expecting his orders. Ad-

mire the divine goodness, be enamoured with humility. Join ejaculatory prayers to common actions. Reflect, that as St. Joseph nourished Christ corporally, so Jesus nourished his Foster-father spiritually, who improved in all virtues, and became a most accomplished saint.

The Colloquy.

OMnipotent God! who *descendest from heaven to bring fire to the earth*, (*St. Luke* xii.) inflame my frozen heart, that I may imitate the virtues of St. Joseph. As a poor wretch waits at the gate of some noble and generous prince, expecting an alms, so I appear before you, wounded in all my senses by sin, and craving a charity in my great calamity. I grieve for what is past, not because I fear, but because I love; nothing has succeeded with me, because I never consulted you. I made you a stranger to all my affairs, and represented them to others, who could not afford any relief. I beg by the intercession of St. Joseph, that I may decline evil and do good, that I may leave the sin-

su

ful track of the broad way, and walk directly towards you. That I may distribute the few remaining hours of my short life, to your honour, and attaining the end for which I was created, that I may admire, praise, and love you, for ever and ever. Amen.

MEDITATION VIIII.

Of St. Joseph's happy departure.

The preparatory Prayer, as in the former Meditation.

First Prelude.

Imagine to see St. Joseph upon his death-bed, our blessed Saviour, and his mother kneeling on each side. How he sweetly rendered his soul to God, was conducted by angels to Limbo, and his body decently interred.

Second Prelude.

Beg grace to lead such a life, as to be favoured on your death-bed, by the protection of Jesus, and the special intercession of Mary and Joseph.

POINT I.

Confider, THAT before the nuptial feaft of Cana in Gallilee, St. Jofeph was vifited with his final ficknefs. *St Epiphan. Hær. 78. Francifcus Locus. Baron,)* He then exercifed, (as he had done thro' the whole courfe of his life) feraphical acts of divine love, and heroic acts of patience and refignation, which the Son of God fuggefted to him. O what a heavenly fcene was it, to behold the fecond Perfon of the moft bleffed Trinity, kneeling on one fide of his bed, and the mother of his Redeemer on the other? Both tenderly thanked him for the conftant care and pains, undertaken fo many years upon their account. St. Jofeph with tears of joy returned humble thanks for the honour they had done him, by acknowledging the difcharge of his duty, and for their affection towards him. He begged, as the laft favour in this world, a bleffing from Chrift's hand, that fills every creature with benediction, and likewife the

powerful

powerful interceffion of his immaculate Spoufe, for a happy paffage to eternity; which being granted with grateful tears, he petitioned like old Simeon to be difmiffed in peace, and wrapt into' an extafy with the love of God, he breathed out his precious foul. Thrice happy death, the reward of a virtuous life. My God! Let my departure be like that of the juft. Infinite goodnefs! infinite power! affift me now, and at the dreadful trial. Let me not be confounded at the hour of death. Ponder alfo how Jefus with his facred hands, clofed the Patriarch's eyes. To deferve a happy death, fhut now your eyes to the world, make fuch timely preparations, as you would wifh to have done, when ftruggling in your agony. Infult over hell by a change of life, fend up afpirations, defiring to be diffolved and to be with Chrift. Be exact in every confeffion, as if it were the laft. Do not fleep in mortal fin, left fudden death feize you, and you be loft eternally. Addrefs St. Jofeph, that you may have the benediction of

Jefus.

Jesus on your death bed, and rejoice with thoughts of being called out of banishment.

POINT II.

Consider, THAT if angels carried the soul of poor Lazarus into Abraham's bosom, a noble choir of those blessed spirits were commanded to conduct and wait on St. Joseph's to Limbo. At his coming thither, they might make use of the high-priest Joachim's words to conquering Judith, and sing, here enters *the glory of Jerusalem, the joy of Israel, and the honour of your people.* This is the soul of great St. Joseph, who governed and supported your Creator thirty years, who was spouse to the mother of God. Reflect how the saved souls of kings, patriarchs and prophets, rejoiced at his entrance, but much more, when he gave an agreeable relation of the birth and life of the long expected Messiah, and that their redemption was near at hand. O my soul! languish for that happy hour, when thy good angel

will conduct thee to hear the transporting invitation, *enter into the joy of
thy Lord.* Obey the angels voice,
exciting you to acts of faith, hope,
love of God, contrition and resignation, that they may be familiar to you
on your death-bed. Reflect on your
former sins, that if you had been called away at such and such a time, you
had been now burning with Cain and
Judas. Give thanks for your preservation, resolve rather to dismiss all that
is dear to you in the world, than divine grace. Consider likewise how
our blessed Saviour and the immaculate Virgin, waited on St. Joseph's
corpse to the place of interment,
(Barradius lib. 6. c. 8.) which was
the valley of Josophat, near the place
where afterwards the blessed Virgin's
body was deposited for some days,
betwixt Mount Sion and Mount Oli-
vet, *(ven, Beda, Bruchardus)* and since
the bodies of several saints have been
preserved from corruption, it is no
rash thought to be of opinion, that our
holy Patriarch was favoured after the
like manner. O precious reliques!
O what:

O what an honour, that God in person should take care of the funeral,
and with his sacred hands place the
body in the sepulchre. Admire the
dignity of St. Joseph. Carry about
you reliques, which terrify devils, and
keep them at distance. Detest no-
velty, shun the dangerous company of
those who cast out words, reflecting
on any practice of the present church
of Christ. Live so that you may
appear with security and joy, in the
valley of Josophat, when Christ comes
to judge the world.

POINT III.

Consider, HOW Christ our Lord,
rising from his sepul-
chre, visited his expecting servants in
Limbo. He took them from thence,
as trophies of his bitter passion, and
whereas *many bodies of saints arose
that had slept,* (St. Mat. xxvii. 52.)
we may not doubt of St. Joseph's
being of that happy number, for it is
piously believed (*St. Bernardin, Tom.
3. Serm. de St. Joseph, Gerson, &c*)
that St. Joseph is both soul and body
glorious

glorious in heaven, although thefe of others arifing at that time might return to their tombs. The Son of God and the holy Patriarch went to vifit the dolorous Mother. O what comfort! What a torrent of joy overflowed the bleffed Virgin's heart, at that glorious apparition of her immortal fon and dear fpoufe. As grief abounded before fo did then confolation. Die with Chrift by mortification, that you may rife with him to a new life. Renounce prefent pleafures, that you may rejoice for ever. Break through all difficulties to open the way out of your loathfome tomb of vice, where you have lain fo long and fo fordidly. Ponder alfo that according to the opinion of many found doctors, St. Jofeph is the moft eminent faint in heaven * next to the bleffed Virgin, and how on the afcenfion-day, our Lord carried up in triumph his Fofter-father, both body

* Suarez p. 3. Tom. 2. Gerfon, Serm. De Nativ. Conf. 4. Bernardin. 4. Part ferm. 12. Cartagene Tom. 1 L. 4. Hom. 1. & 9. Ifidor 4. Part. cap. 2 Sego. Serm. de S. Jofeph, & alii.

and foul, and placed him on a glorious throne, next to that prepared for the Mother of God. What joy did he then experience for paft fufferings? What glory for contempt? What a refplendent crown for purity of life? O my fluggifh foul! take pains like St. Jofeph in ferving Chrift, that you may be rewarded with him; call frequently to mind thofe divine words of our Redeemer, *what doth it profit a man if he gains the whole world, and fuftains the damage of his foul.* (*St. Mat.* xvi.) the enjoyment is fhort, and the punifhment eternal. On the contrary, faithful fervants of the Omnipotent, have tranfient trials, fhort afflictions, whether exterior or interior, but they gain a never ending and happy kingdom. Say often to yourfelf, what can feparate me from the love of my God? Not all the menances of cruel man, nor all the malice of hell. I will love my omnipotent Creator, I will love my moft merciful Redeemer, I will love my gracious Sanctifier, purely for their own fakes, I will love them eternally.

The

The Colloquy.

O Moſt glorious Patriarch, my dear Patron! *Bleſſed are the eyes that ſee, what you now ſee.* I confide with holy Job, through the infinite merits of Chriſt, and by your powerful interceſſion, that *in my fleſh I ſhall ſee God my Saviour.* Stretch out, for your unworthy client, thoſe happy hands, which carried ſo often, and provided for the Son of God. Petition that I may live, as I wiſh to die, always in the divine favour. I moſt humbly beg that you will prevail with your immaculate Spouſe, to join in prayer with you, that I her unworthy ſuppliant, may be a ſaved ſoul, & make one of the number of the elect. With profound humility, I invite you both to be preſent with me at the dreadful hour of my death, when my laſt grateful words ſhall be, with my parting breath, to invoke the ſacred names of Jeſus, Mary, Joſeph; and having ſatisfied divine juſtice for manifold tranſgreſſions in the ſcorching flames

of

of purgatory, the very moment that I
shall be admitted to the beatifical vifion, I will proftrate myfelf before the
throne of mercy, and I will fay; O
my God! your charity was infinite,
and your goodnefs incomprehenfible,
to bring into this celeftial manfion, a
vile worm of the earth. I deferved
to have been now raging with repro-
bate fouls in unquenchable fire, and
not to be an eye-witnefs of fo great
glory, but your mercy is above all
your works. Moft facred Trinity!
my prefent happinefs is moft dear
unto me, becaufe this tranfporting
felicity was perfected by your bounti-
ful grace and favour, more than by
my poor merits co-operating, to take
poffeffion of heaven. I will then addrefs the Mother of God, and you
her glorious Spoufe, as alfo the nine
choirs of angels, and all bleffed fouls,
to join with me in acts of thankfgiving, to God the Father, God the Son,
and God the Holy Ghoft, and for
ever and ever. *Amen.*

CONTENTS.

www.ingramcontent.com/pod-product-compliance
Lightning Source LLC
Chambersburg PA
CBHW020009030726
47500CB00002B/507